The Therapist's Cat

The Therapist's Cat

Stephanie Sorrell

Winchester, UK
Washington, USA

First published by Soul Rocks Books, 2012
Soul Rocks Books is an imprint of John Hunt Publishing Ltd., Laurel House, Station Approach,
Alresford, Hants, SO24 9JH, UK
office1@o-books.net
www.o-books.com

For distributor details and how to order please visit the 'Ordering' section on our website.

Text copyright: Stephanie Sorrell 2010

ISBN: 978 1 84694 847 3

A CIP catalogue record for this book is available from the British Library.

Design: Stuart Davies

Printed in the UK by CPI Antony Rowe
Printed in the USA by Edwards Brothers Malloy

We operate a distinctive and ethical publishing philosophy in all
areas of our business, from our global network of authors to
production and worldwide distribution.

Disclaimer

The author does not necessarily share the same views as the feline character, Moo. But as time has passed this is changing.

Acknowledgments

This work is dedicated to Minnie Moo, the real author of this work and who stayed with me for 23 years.

Thank you to Alice Grist, of Soul Rocks, who saw Moo's potential.

Thank you to Hanne Jahr who painstakingly lived and breathed this work and offered support throughout.

Gratitude for Janice Savage for reading and helping to proofread it with her practised eye.

Thank you to Jenny Dent and Michelle Lovric who, despite their hectic schedules, read and endorsed this work.

Chapter One

Really, it had all started eight years ago.

At a time when I should have been convalescing and, perhaps, taking on less work, I made a decision to go on a grueling expedition to the Himalayas. It was one of those things I had always planned to do some time in the future when I was still youngish, but never got around to. What brought the desire fast forward was the diagnosis that the lump that had appeared almost overnight in my neck wasn't benign as I expected, but a malignant tumor. Not only that, but the cancer was particularly aggressive and was in danger of metastasizing if I hadn't got shot of it. Although they couldn't locate any primary cancer, they weren't taking any chances, especially as cancer existed on both sides of my family history. The constriction in my throat that had drawn my attention to it, was dangerously near the oesophagus and I underwent surgery almost immediately. It all happened so quickly that I didn't have time to process any feelings around it, and afterwards I was so numb and shattered from the diagnosis and surgery that my emotions still stayed somewhere in the background.

But then, after being discharged from High Dependency Unit (HDU) where my life had hung in the balance after a respiratory arrest, triggered off by an allergy to some drug, the reality had set in. I felt as though I was encased in concretized fear. Panic attacks plagued me night and morning leaving me awash in cold clammy sweat and my heart pounding hollowly like a kudos drum.

I had cancer. At the age of 36 I had my first real wake-up call. Longevity wasn't something I could look upon as my divine right. If I hadn't had that tumor removed when I did, I could have died. Simple as that. It had been a particularly virulent strain of cancer, the consultant had told me. Like a silent predator it had stalked me down, so diligently and silently, that when it pounced I hardly knew what had hit me.

Surgery had left more than a superficial cosmetic scar. It had cut deep into the layers of my psyche.

You see, up until then, I'd enjoyed a sense of omnipotence, despite a glitch in the efficacy of my neurotransmitters. A glitch that had become deeply embedded in the genetic matrix of my family bloodline. Somehow, I had come to terms with the crazy swings of mood from the dizzy ebullient highs to the plummeting down and down into lows that knew no depths and which dangerously framed my bipolar disorder. These hazardous mood swings which could snatch me off that peak of intellectual brilliance and catapult me across the millwheel of suicidal depression, grinding me up into a heap of desiccated dreams, as it had my father. He had successfully committed suicide when I was 12. Now there was a secondary glitch within my genetic framework in the form of malignancy and tumors, which had descended from my mother's bloodline and claimed her life at the age of 42. Over the years, I had come to accept lithium and the other medley of mood stabilizers, antipsychotics and anti-depressants as vital to my well-being. But that didn't stop me from being ambivalent towards medication. At worst, it undermined everything I believed and practiced: that we were creatures of free will that had the potential to become autonomous beings. At best, it kept me on an even keel, not descending too low or ascending too high. Medication made me normal but, by the same token, it violated my autonomy. But with this new diagnosis of my body's fallibility, I realised I was fatally flawed. Time was running out. If I didn't pick life up by the 'short and curlies', then I wouldn't have any 'short and curlies' left after chemotherapy!

When I planned my trip to the Himalayas it had, momentarily, crossed my mind that, if the worst came to the worst, I could even kill myself there. Once up in the mountains, proper medical care would be several days journey away and a lethal cocktail of drugs would do the trick. But then conscience would creep in and I would think of the other people in my team whose experience of the Himalayas would be forever tarnished by the suicide of one of its members. I should know. I had trained in psychotherapy and my eight year long practise had made me aware of the emotional carnage suicide could leave for others to clean up. One that could last years.

One of my long-standing clients was still experiencing the emotional fallout of a close friend's suicide ten years previously. Josie was still wrestling under the weight of guilt feelings, blame, and resentment. My act could traumatize my fellow members for years afterwards. For many, this trek was a one off opportunity of a lifetime. What right had I to ruin other peoples experience? Momentarily, I toyed with the idea of hurling myself off one of the slippery precipices with a 10,000 feet drop on either side. A supposed accident rather than a suicidal act would be more easily digested. But always there would be someone who would carry the blame for the loss of life even though the trekking company's small print absolved them of death by accident. But I knew blame would sit well with our trek leader, simply because she was female and guilt sat easily with the feminine psyche of our race. Alongside this, another more sobering thought crept in: supposing I didn't do it properly? I left myself maimed for the rest of my life? Thinking, in fact, didn't help. I would just back myself into endless corners that I couldn't find a way out of.

Yet, my trip to the Himalayas, instead of reinforcing Freud's death instinct to end everything, gave me new reasons to live. It wasn't just the stunning beauty of the place, the clear unspoilt panorama of peaks that pierced the skyline; it was the spirit of the place. There was something about the white silence and majesty of the landscape that juxtaposed sharply with the poverty of the towns and villages that nestled precariously amidst the breathless panorama. The dust tracks of Pokhara alongside the dazzling brilliance of its dyes and spices in the market square contrasted with the stunning beauty of Machapuchare, the fishtail mountain that towered majestically above. The bright iridescence of saffron and chili powder in their Hessian sacks would come and go, as would the people, but the rock and glacial beauty would outlive everything here today. Somehow, although I couldn't articulate it in words, I was part of that too.

Someone else reinforced my reason to live.

This was Emmanuella. Emmie for short; a twenty-three-year-old art student who had taken a year out from her degree course to travel and spend the £20,000 legacy her grandfather had left her. Emmie, because of her mixed race parents, one being Swedish, the other Italian, had striking blue, almost turquoise eyes, high cheekbones, and natural olive skin with a leonine mane of golden ringlets that she ran her fingers through when she was describing something from the past. Her eyelashes were long, dark silken fringes. Medium build with nicely rounded proportions, like most women I met, she wasn't as generous when describing her physical appearance. She was outspoken and direct, but moody too. The most adorable thing about her was her lisp, dimples and the way her nose crinkled when she laughed. When she talked to you it was as if, for her, everyone and everything else in the world had vanished. Whoever she talked to became her world whether they liked it or not. I think most people liked it because she was such a vibrant attractive person to be around. We hit it off fairly quickly and hung out together a lot.

But two days into our relationship, she began to act very strangely, hedging towards the back of the trekking party instead of steaming ahead as she usually did. But when I offered to fall into step with her, she snapped at me, so I left her, not wanting to jeopardize our budding relationship. I moved forward into the middle of the expedition, glancing back every now and then to look at the dizzying landscape about me, checking out what was going on with Emmie, who was trudging now, head down, scowling at everything. Yet, unable to stop myself, I dropped behind with her again. "Leave me!" she hissed. "I'll be okay. Oh – you haven't got anything in your pack to eat, a sweet or fruit or something. I'm starving..."

"Sure...If that will bring a smile to your face," I rummaged around in my pocket and brought out the bland chocolate ration we were given which was unlike any chocolate I had ever tasted. Made by some obscure Indian company I was sure that it had well passed its sell-by-date.

She wolfed it down, muttering, "You just go ahead...I'll be all right in a sec. Can you tell them to stop somewhere soon? I need to pee."

I waved to one of the porters and they motioned to Jodie to make a stop who, in turn, glanced anxiously at her watch. "We'll have to make it fairly quick, we need to set up camp in the next hour. Tenzing says there's bad weather ahead."

I glanced up at the clear blue skies. "Where?" I responded with naïve arrogance.

"It might not be visible yet, but its there all right," Jodie finished, glancing across at the porters. "These natives have a second instinct when it comes to the weather. When Tenzing says there's going to be a storm, then he means it."

"A storm!" Gerry, an older know-it-all at my elbow echoed. "What sort of a storm?"

Jodie and Tenzing exchanged words and I could see by the Nepalese head sherpa's body language that he was tense. Unusual for him. Small, wiry with a round face and eyes that looked as if they were always laughing, he was the epitome of a relaxed person.

"Okay – I'm going." Emmie called, scuttling off in search of a rock to hide her modesty, while the rest of us waited in tense silence.

The minutes seemed to drag and several times I looked up nervously at the sky, already imagining that storm clouds were beginning to flank the horizon. Although she hadn't got far to go and the place where we would be setting camp looked deceptively near, the way to it was steep, full of dangerous precipices that, on either side, pitched down into 8,000 feet drops. I was aware of ambivalent feelings inside me. On one level, I felt a spiralling sense of exhilaration as if a part of me was feeding off the drama of what lay about us and ahead of us. On another level, I felt unease as if something that I couldn't quite fathom was steadily creeping up on me, ready to pounce. I heard an edgy interchange between Jodie and Tampa and then Jodie looked back at me. "We have to get going now!"

I read more in her agitated gaze. The 'now' said: 'I can't allow one person to jeopardize the safety of the whole trekking party. It's tough… but that's how it is here…'

"I'll go and look for her," I heard myself say.

I knew in which direction Emmie had gone and the rest revealed itself in the spiral pattern of her boot tread. I found her behind an overhanging cornice; squatting, fully engrossed in pushing the needle into her arm, her face white with taut concentration. *Holy shit!* a voice inside me sounded. And then again, *holy shit!*

I drew back noiselessly, not wanting her to know that I had seen her, but aware of conflicting emotions raging in me. And I thought, "God, a druggie and a storm brewing in the Himalayas!"

Besides that, I was aware of a mounting sense of exhilaration inside me at the raw danger we were in. Emotionally, I felt close to the edge of something I had to keep a tight reign on. But now wasn't the time to deal with what I had witnessed. Edging back behind the invisibility of the rock, I called urgently. "Emmie – there's a storm brewing, we have to leave *now!*"

"Just coming."

Suddenly, she was beside me, pulling down her sleeve, adjusting her jacket and I noticed the tense aura had shifted. The 'spikiness' had gone as she hurried to catch me up. We trudged in silence, partly because I didn't want to stir up emotional stuff by referring to what I had witnessed and mainly because there was a sense that the sky was pressing down upon us. In the rear with Emmie, I could see everyone in front, heads bent forwards, shoulders braced. No words were spoken, and between us, there was a deep focus on the process ahead, which kept the panic in abeyance. In my counseling work, I often came up against this countertransference in my clients when we had swung to close to a black hole in their psyche. Palpably, I experienced it as a steady wall of covert concentration, protecting the fragile emotions from being overwhelmed by any of the three terrors: *annihilation, isolation* and *freedom*. There was an indelible lifeline to sanity entrenched deep in the western psyche: 'keep busy, keep focused' on the bolt hole whatever that be, but usually it was in the form of work. This was an unstated mantra where the western population slotted inside each other like Russian dolls. Work upon work upon work. In the beginning, the survival mantra underpinned the work one. But, this was no longer so for most people, it was the fear of what lay beyond and outside work, which drove people frenetically, forward and kept their heads down from admiring the views around them like us trekkers.

Beyond the work drive was a terrifying abyss that kept the majority of the westernized world in shackles. The only agreed 'escape' was in the form of long flight holidays. Alcohol infused holidays abounded alongside an abundance of other recreational drugs. For others, it was activity holidays like this. As long as we all kept striving and achieving, that terrifying abyss became subliminal, just resting below the threshold of consciousness. In short, westernized people cannot rest. We were like hamsters on one of those bright plastic treadmills, running on and on until we dropped into a comatose exhaustion. Even 'spiritual' holidays were suspect with the overloaded programs of walking and sitting meditation, growth and creativity workshops. 'Nothingness' and 'entropy' were words that few but the dedicated veterans in Buddhism and Zen could openly embrace. Tasters of which were given in open meditations and open days where people from the 'outside' came together within to rekindle a sense of belonging and community rather than any deeper issues. Once this belonging was assuaged, the thoughts surged on…If Emmie beside me was tripping with whatever she was on, I was too on the rarefied air at 13,000 feet. Basically I was high up, feeling high. I checked myself, scanning through my pharmaceutical lifesavers. I'd dropped the lithium with my Psyche's advice. It didn't work well with changes in altitude and it was really only any good if there was a third party to monitor my emotional temperament. Experience had shown me again and again that I couldn't trust myself when it came to monitoring moods and medication. I had tried to compensate for the lithium defect by upping the mood stabilizers, carbemazepine, but that was making me sick and dizzy in the high altitude and I had been forced to drop down on those too.

"Hey, are you okay?" Emmie was at my side, pulling me back from that internal abyss and I could hear the lightness back in her voice. "You look as if you're a zillion miles away."

I came to and stopped myself from asking what the hell she had been up to behind that rock. "Yeah, I'm fine…but the weather's not."

Squalls of sulfurous snow laden cloud were already obscuring Machapuchare and Annapurna. The narrow path we were negotiating was icy underneath the powdery layer of recently fallen snow. Our boots compounded it, making it more slippery. Instead of moving faster we were in fact moving slower. Jodie and Tenzing shouted at each other and although I couldn't make sense of the interchange, I could hear the panic behind the sounds.

With supreme effort, I silenced my thoughts and held down the mounting exuberance. It was like one of those unwound golf balls that we hid in the desk at school. However hard we tried to muffle the bouncing, it kept on, boom…boom…boom…Here, I could at least tamp down the panic, but I couldn't stop it. We trudged in single file, not stopping, drawing on reserves of energy, which everyone except me, didn't know we had.

Then we were up, the porters already ahead of us were putting up the tents, shouting to each other through the first squalls of snow. Only Tenzing was helping one of the others to put up the food tent, but after a period of watching the canvas flapping like some big green monster, they abandoned it and waved us on to a deserted old building which could have been anything from a school, a climber's hut to even a Hindu chapel. We all gathered inside the windowless rooms, drawing blankets around us while Jodie instructed us what to do.

"This could be a bit hairy tonight!" she warned. "As long as you follow my instructions you'll be fine…Right, rule number one," she indicated soberly with her index finger, "no wandering off on your own. Once the visibility goes, everywhere outside the tent is dangerous. If you have to pee, do it in a bottle or stick your bum out of the tent." She raised her index finger. "Drink plenty…You're at high altitude, and your body's having to work extra hard. You'll feel tired and slow because of the altitude, so don't expect any miracles…No taking pictures. And rule three: try not to worry," she smiled wanly. "Tenzing, myself and all these sherpas have been through this before…Many times…We'll do the best we can to work for your safety."

The sherpas gave a squeal of delight as the wood and leaf kindling caught fire and the welcome smell of wood smoke filled the icy building.

"At least we can have tea now," someone cheered and there was an interchange of relieved sounds of agreement.

Momentarily, the dark wall of fear eased into the background as everyone stared at the blackened kettle, waiting for the steam to rise and reach as near boiling as the altitude would allow.

"Right," Jodie was on her feet, as what passed for tea got handed around in ancient metal beakers. "When you've had your drink, get your head down for a couple of hours in the tent and we'll meet later for supper...But first," she added as people began to fidget, "you all need to collect a few big stones or rocks to hold the tent down tonight. We don't have storms here, as much as blizzards..."

"Blizzards!" several of the female members echoed.

"Don't be too alarmed..." came Jodie's reassurance, "I've been caught in several myself – and although I might look older than my twenty one years, I'm still here!"

That got us all laughing, relieved to find something to centre our anxiety on.

"Oh," she added. "And help each other. Out here it's not every person to themselves...We move as a team. We can only be as strong as our weakest link and that weak link is as strong as we all make it. Okay?"

"Is there something I can eat?" Emmie called out, unable to conceal a strident edge to her voice. "I'm starving, I can't wait two hours."

"Well – that's what it's like up here...There are no fast food places round here," a trekker, Gerry, whom we called Old-Know-It-All, called out smugly. "The twentieth century hasn't made it this far."

I frowned with concern as I took in Emmie's blanched face, her skin was wan and clammy, her pupils dilated. "Come on," she snapped, "get me something to eat, for pity sake!"

"Are you diabetic?" Jodie asked frowning.

Emmie nodded.

"You should have said," Jodie countered.

"I know," Emmie was beginning to tremble. "I thought that I

wouldn't be allowed to come if I said I was…I brought plenty of dried fruit, but I've eaten it all." She sank down, pulling off her gloves and scarf and her shoulders shook. "I'm sorry."

"Well there's no use fretting now," Jodie said, spontaneously putting an arm round the girl. "Has anyone got anything high in carbs that she can eat? A piece of bread, fruit, banana?"

Old Know-It-All came forward and held out his chocolate bar which Emmie snatched, tearing off the wrapper shakily and stuffing several pieces in her mouth. Someone else came forward with a couple of boiled sweets. Another presented a Fisherman's Friend.

Why hadn't I picked up on that? Now it all made sense! Her moodiness, her almost starving need to have something to eat. I felt ashamed of myself for jumping to conclusions, for not seeing. Driven by an overwhelming sense of guilt, I collected rocks for everyone and personally made sure the tent Emmie was sharing with a girl from Belgium was held down tightly. While she recovered inside her tent, I stomped about restlessly. Angry with my own self-importance, my judgmental attitude. What if she hadn't said anything?

The vicious lash of storm driven snow against my face, taking my breath away, forced me to concentrate on survival issues. Finding rocks and carrying them back was easier said than done. The rocks which might have been visible minutes before, were hidden beneath the driving storm. The effort of walking and breathing at high altitude in the face of the storm was more challenging than I'd realized. I could feel my heart thumping hard to compensate for the decreased oxygen level even though I was barely doing anything.

Making an effort to absolve myself of guilt, I worked relent-lessly to help Emmie with her collection of rocks; packing them hard against the canvas, which was the only protection we had against the blizzard. I collapsed inside, gulping down my ration of water and trying to force myself to stay awake, concentrating hard on my own survival. I had read so many stories where mountaineers in the first stage of hypothermia became sleepy and muddle headed as their body temperature plummeted. Mentally, I ran through the symptoms: drowsiness, confusion, shivering, and shortness of breath. I was moderately clear in my head and I wasn't shivering and the drowsiness could just as easily be caused by high altitude.

It seemed that no sooner had I run through the symptoms, Jodie was shaking me awake. "What's wrong?" I asked blearily.

"Supper's ready," she said.

"Already?" I squinted at my watch, both shocked and ashamed to find that it was six o'clock in the evening. I had been asleep for two hours. I thought of Emmie. " Is everyone okay?" I asked.

"Yeah…Apart from a general reluctance to make it to the food tent, and some nausea, which is perfectly natural at this altitude. That's why it's important that we move around, drink and eat." Although Jodie was shouting, it was still hard to hear what she was saying. "Can I have a word with you. I want to talk about Emmie."

"Sure. Is she all right?"

"The problem is she's diabetic. If she'd mentioned that before she came, we could have been able to allow for that. My brother's diabetic so I know a little about the problems that can emerge in extreme conditions. She keeps her insulin at body temperature on a belt round her waist, but if her body temperature drops, that's not going to help. Insulin is very sensitive to changes in temperature and she's more susceptible to frost bite, can you watch out for her?"

"Sure…. What do I look for?"

"Oh…. confusion, clamminess, irritability, although, at this altitude," she added grimly, "it's easy to confuse diabetic symptoms with hypothermia or altitude sickness. The thing is, she might try to hide it from you if she thinks it's going to jeopardize the expedition. You'll just have to have your antennae on full alert."

Emmie was already in the food tent and she smiled at me wanly, her features tired and strained like everybody else's. We ate the stew and bread in silence, the usual humor and bravura absent, all of us concerned with the near future and our personal safety. Jodie, looking as tired as the rest of us, did not let any underlying worries show and gave us firm practical advice. "The storm can go on for hours, but with a bit of luck it'll die out by morning so we can travel. At the worst, if it doesn't, we have enough food to last us a couple of days...As I said, drink plenty and move around. But..." She raised her index finger, "remember rule number one...Do not wander at all from your tent. This is because the visibility is so poor, you cannot take that risk. Remember there are precipices that plunge straight into 8,000 foot drops."

After supper I lost sight of Emmie as I made my way back to the tent. It was hard to see or hear anything clearly in the storm. Concerned for Emmie, I made my way to her tent, but my flashlight just revealed the turned up sleeping bag, a notebook and rucksack. Perhaps she had gone to the toilet, but when I called outside the toilet tent and there was no sign of her, I experienced the first flutter of panic. Supposing she had wandered off, got lost and lay in a diabetic coma somewhere? If I didn't find her soon, I'd have to notify Jodie – then what? What could we do amidst this storm raging on? Where could we go? What were a few flares amidst the raw galvanic interplay of the elements?

Stopping by the other tents, I poked my head in and asked if anyone had seen Emmie. The response was negative and I was about to go looking for Jodie when I had a hunch and returned to my own tent.

A trail of partially covered footsteps with the spiral indentation led up to my tent and, as I pulled back the flap and saw Emmie huddled inside, bending over a book reading, I was surprised at the savage intensity of relief as it swept through me.

"Here," I said, handing her my flashlight. "It might be easier to read with this."

"Do you mind?" she asked a little nervously. "I just don't feel safe in my tent. I feel safe with you."

"Of course I don't mind," I gabbled a little too eagerly. "I've been looking for you, I'm glad you're okay and it's a lot cozier with two...I mean temperature wise."

"That's what I thought," she said, relaxing. "I'll go get my sleeping bag and gear."

"No, let me," I insisted, "I don't mind. Really."

I was gone before she could protest, and my heart seemed lighter and once again I was in touch with that exuberance.

Then we were sitting in my tent, talking by the flashlight while the storm howled outside. It was sort of surreal, us sitting there, sharing intimate parts of our lives in such close proximity when, a few days ago, we had been strangers. Outside, the blizzard howled and grumbled like some crazed animal. Every now and then, when the wind changed direction and the 'grumbling animal' went off to howl somewhere else, the voices of our neighbors reached us. We listened to the drift of words.

"We only have enough food for three days – and what about that diabetic girl?" A man's voice reached us, followed by that of a woman. "I'm scared, Victor. I'm too young to die." There was a silence and then; "You're not going to die, Annie."

"God – it's serious, isn't it?" Emmie breathed.

"Well – you've been dicing with death with your diabetes coming up here, that doesn't help."

"I know, I'm sorry."

She grinned at my expression. "It's okay. I'm not on my own, am I? We've both been dicing with death, me with my diabetes, you with your bipolar disorder. They're both serious and life threatening illnesses."

"True. How are you feeling in yourself?"

"I'm not too bad considering. The carbs helped and I checked my blood sugar levels an hour ago. It was 6.4, which is good. What about you?"

"A bit high, actually." I admitted.

We both giggled at the words. "That's true," she said, "but I'm high too with you."

"I'm a bit too exuberant."

"What does that mean for you?"

"It means I could quite easily go over the edge."

She giggled again. "That's true. Sorry, I'm not laughing at you but at the situation and I'm nervous – what's going to happen to us, Pete?"

"D'you mean the blizzard?"

"Partly…"

"What else?"

She paused to run her fingers through her hair and I caught the flash of gold in the light. "Between us – what's going to happen?"

"What do you want to happen?" I asked, aware of the charged atmosphere inside. We were sitting so close together that I could feel her breath on my cheek, warm and fragrant with mint and something floral.

"I don't know. Nothing – too fast, I guess. What about you?"

"I'm the same. I don't want to spoil things. Spoil what we've got."

She grinned. "Then we're the same. Are you in a relationship?"

I shook my head. "Not at the moment. It's hard to be in a stable relationship with someone with bipolar disorder," I admitted. "When I'm on a high I become very full of myself – in fact so much so that everyone else gets squeezed out. In my mind I become inviolable, omnipotent."

"What about when you're low?"

"I get suicidal like my dad. He killed himself."

"That doesn't mean that you will. Like my mum had diabetes and had heart problems, it doesn't mean I will."

The wild animal of the storm returned, ripping at the tent flaps, buffeting the canvas so that it ballooned out, then just as quickly deflated.

We talked until Emmie was too tired to talk anymore. I watched her slipping into a relaxed sleep despite the storm raging outside. Listening to her even breathing, I gazed down at her before switching off the torch. I was grateful for Emmie's company then, her body warmth through the sleeping bag. Although I'd been glad at first that, unlike the other trekkers, I had my tent to myself, I knew that being on my own for any length of time with my emotional instability could be dangerous, life threatening even. Thankfully, I remembered to take my mood stabilizers, knowing that if I didn't I would live to regret it.. Too much exuberance would drive me out to confront the hungry animal, challenging it with my presence because I would believe that I was the stronger of the two of us. And... it was good to have someone to look after.

By the time I fell asleep, it was the early hours of the morning.

But when I awoke to light again, it seemed only moments later and it took me a while to get my bearings because of the unearthly silence after the last few hours. I shook my head, wondering if I was still dreaming. But no, here was Emmie asleep beside me, sleeping bag pulled over her head, hair falling in a golden cascade about the duvet. And the light.....It was so bright!

Was there a moon? Then the skies must be clear. Was this dawn in the Himalayas? I moved carefully, silently towards the entrance, unzipping the inner lining of the tent and peering out through the small opening between the ties stitched into the outer flap. I pulled on my boots and laced them, then pushed my way out into the cold air. It wasn't dawn. No sun. And the view...

Peak upon peak stippled the horizon like icing sugar steeples on a Christmas cake. The one directly ahead, I recognized as

Annapurna. Just a plume circled it like a smoke ring. The snow must have been soft and powdery because my feet made scarcely a sound as I walked. Surely it would be okay if I took a little wander? The visibility was good and I felt so alive, full of energy. I looked back at the tents, most of the canvases covered in snow so that they looked like a row of pure white hummocks. Was I cold? No.

I'm on my way to you...

I spun round at the clear female voice.

Nothing. No one.

I checked myself, heart hammering wildly. Was I psychotic? High, yes. But not psychotic.

We will be together again soon. The voice that seemed to come from everywhere reached into me.

Swallowing, I stared at Annapurna, at the smoke ring that was becoming incandescent with a light which steadily coalesced into a definable shape. I became aware of warm fur that thrummed strangely and a feline form with emerald eyes that seemed to reach right into me. I checked myself thinking I must be dreaming.

"Who are you?" I whispered. "What are you?"

The form shimmered as I spoke and I saw the tail, the paws the whiskers, superimposed on the mountain. But then the form seemed to metamorphose from being distinctly feline, to the human shape of a woman. I shook my head and rubbed my eyes. Now, I really had to be hallucinating or else I was seriously deluding myself!

*Peter...*The voice called melodiously, *don't you remember me?*

"No," I responded in a tone that was strangely unconvincing, "I can't say that I do."

You saved my life...In another incarnation...Another time...That creates an enduring bond that transverses all incarnations in matter."

"I..."

The voice was faint, and the form was dissolving, as was the light. "Hang on," I heard myself grunt and whispered, "who are you? Don't go…"

As the light faded and my surroundings darkened, I began to shiver as the icy cold reached me. I felt Emmie moving next to me, felt her breath against my cheek, her voice in my ear. "Pete – are you okay?"

"Yeah!"

"You were calling out in your sleep.."

My lips searched for hers, welcoming her warmth, her physical presence and sometime later, I went back to sleep, wanting and needing the oblivion it offered.

Chapter Two

You humans always think in terms of punishment and retribution,
loss and success... But you can't measure the working out of these
things in that way. It's too mechanistic... These things happen
because it's the way of the earth, the Mooisphere, the Great Purr...
Gospel of Moo

If I am totally honest, a lot more went on during those two weeks
in the Himalayas than I could possibly give credit to here. But
because it all manifested in another geographical place and on
what I can only describe as another level of consciousness, a
surreal one, I have stored much of the content somewhere else,
like a USB memory stick which I only have access to every now
and then. And yet, it's a level of being that energizes me when I
am in touch with it. I can well understand the need for people
(namely, my clients) to cut off from transpersonal experiences
and encase themselves in worldly injunctions of grounding
themselves in matter and materialism. As I can understand the
enticing pull that these otherworldly experiences have over the
impoverished Western psyche. The fact that drugs have become
rife in the West, is a symptom of a need to return to our Source,
or access it in some way. Needless to say, my experience in the
Himalayas has enabled me to understand some of my patients
more; the yearning for a more spiritual context to their life.

One of the things I discovered in my training to be a
psychotherapist was that you can only go as deep with your
clients as you have been yourself. If a therapist hasn't navigated
the depths themselves they cannot 'hold' their client in the way
they need to be held. The therapist, out of personal discomfort,
will steer the session onto familiar ground, leaving the client
'unheard' and 'unseen' in a place the therapist refuses to travel.
Unless the client can be witnessed and accepted in that dark

fathomless place, they can never fully 'move on'. Their pain will always call them back to explore and be heard in that place so that they become re-wounded again and again. The only way through is to make a commitment to another therapist, one who can navigate those depths and heights for that matter and embrace them in their client. But things are never as easy as that unless both client and therapist are wise enough to know this and strong enough to implement these changes.

In most cases, client and therapist become enmeshed in an unconscious consensus not to explore those dangerous uncharted depths. And so history repeats itself over and over until the brave therapist and even braver client chooses to break the 'spell' by speaking out for the unspoken…Very dangerous ground!

Needless to say, when I returned from that trek, I was dangerously 'high' despite the mood stabilizers. Thank God I had an observing 'I' which could boldly challenge the deliriously happy state I was in. But it wasn't strong enough to prevent Emmie moving in with me. And of course, life in the normal everyday world with washing up, food, shopping, running out of toilet paper, struggling to pay bills after having spent too much, impinges darkly on any relationship, whether that relationship was forged in the Himalayan peaks or the Australian outback.

But despite my fragility of being, I had to admit that something had lingered over from the trek. From that night after the blizzard, when I'd stepped out of that tent, I'd come in touch with a sense of well being, a soul warmth, if you like. It was as if I was clothed in a security blanket. I thought at first this was Emmie's presence, but it was more than that. All I can say was that it was as if…

I was enfolded in fur. If I closed my eyes I could almost see and feel it, warm and animal-like.

But then I would see Fly's lead behind the kitchen door, his bowls at the bottom of the walk-in pantry. I know I should have got rid of them before I'd gone on my trek, but I hadn't the heart to. Any more than I'd had the heart to get another Border collie as a replacement. I had begun to lose Fly at the same time as I had my cancer diagnosis. By the time I had completed my hospital treatment, he had slipped away. I had read somewhere that animals can take on their owner's physical condition in an empathic selfless act of devotion. I had read about it happening, but until Fly had the same diagnosis as me, I wouldn't have believed it. But still a more sober part of me relegated that experience to coincidence. Then I would feel a shadow move across my heart, as if in believing that, I was dishonoring Fly's illness in some way.

Returning to the empty house, I was glad of Emmie's presence, her company.

I was resentful of it too. I had lived too long on my own to be in a 24/7 relationship. Emmie had moved in during the Christmas holidays and, very wisely, had deliberated jettisoning her university education and possibly ending up without a job, which is enough to try any relationship. We were together two weeks, and from the start, after the initial excitement and physical attraction, we quickly collapsed into the least likeable aspects of our selves. Mine was a selfish 'bachelorhood' where, apparently, I was self-obsessed and therapy obsessed. Emmie's was her total unpredictability and mess in the form of items of clothing, make-up and vitamin pills strewn round the house. She was, by nature, flamboyantly artistic and untidy, I was anally fixated where everything had to be in its self-appointed place. Although to be fair, being anally fixated came with being depressed and low when I needed to be in control of what seemed to be a disorderly world. When I was high, I tended towards oral fixation where I gorged deeply on the fruits of every life experience. In between the staggering heights and the vertiginous drops I believed I was normal, whatever that was.

Being anally fixated in the midst of someone who is orally

fixated, as I believed Emmie was most of the time with her untidiness and love of life, is not a good mix.

When a love relationship begins to flounder and, in this case, the pair of us couldn't bridge the gaps in communication, it is natural to bring in something from outside or create 'another' in the form of a baby, a new house, a holiday or new course, job or toy.

And that was when Moo came in...

After another night where I had moved into the spare room, I awoke with a deep sense of well-being and the sort of peace I hadn't felt in a long time. Again, I experienced that sense of being cocooned in something soft – like fur, living fur.

Realizing I had my first client today after a six week sabbatical from client work; I emptied my bladder and put the coffee maker on. I had an hour to ready myself before my new client came for an initial session. My friend, Michelle, who worked in underprivileged areas on the Moss Side Estate, had put him in touch with me. All I knew was that his name was Kevin, and he was a self-harmer. If the session went well and the boy agreed to more sessions, a contract would be drawn up and the National Health Service would foot the bill.

"I know you said you liked a challenge," Michelle had said. "I have to be honest with you in saying that you are the last resort for Kevin."

"Gee thanks," I had grunted. "There's nothing like rubbing my nose in it after I come back from my holiday!"

"You've been back two weeks," she had reminded me, "and we both know the places you can go in the winter."

"You're right," I agreed. "I should thank you."

Michelle and I had trained together at the same Institute. She was a social worker and had a lot of clients recommended to her for psychotherapy. Ones that she couldn't treat, or who needed a male therapist, she would pass onto me. In short, Michelle accounted for 60% of my clientele. Many people who didn't glimpse anything behind her professional expertise regarded her as a workaholic. Few saw her warmth and empathy apart from her more broken clients. Even fewer glimpsed the deep well of pain that lay behind her solid working front. Now, too old to have children, she had spent twenty years trying to have children by any means possible. One night stands, IVF and finally adoption after her body clock was beginning to falter, but even that was denied her. "All I ever wanted was a child," she had groaned to me. "And I am surrounded by people having babies, dropping out of them like sturgeon eggs!"

But we both knew the dark wall of guilt that overshadowed her every failur€e and loss. Pregnant at sixteen and lacking any parental support, she had had an abortion. And spent the rest of her life regretting it; believing that she was being punished for that act which seemed so sensible at the time. My assurances that she was the only one punishing herself, fell on plugged ears. She worked her penance in the seething furnace of her Catholic upbringing in her never-ending backlog of social work.

"Let me know how it goes with Kevin," she said.

"Will do," I promised. "Over a brew."

The training program had revealed masses of clever competent people of all ages, shapes and sizes, each carrying personal baggage of regret, guilt and self-punishment. I was no longer surprised by anything I heard in my therapy room. As time went by, my uncompromising mindsets around religion began to fragment and change. Buddha was right about suffering and that everyone suffered. Suffering wasn't just about living in socially and geographically impoverished areas, or being prey to mental and physical disability and torture. It was just as much about the more covert ways we are capable of torturing ourselves, and each other. The material wealth that everyone craved as a panacea for all their discomfort, disguised huge watersheds of pain; childhood trauma, sexual anomalies and entanglements ranging from closeted homosexuality to masochism and sadism. No one was exempt from their own watershed of suffering or inflicting pain covertly on others through the decisions and choices they made.

Laying a couple of slices of bread in the toaster, I paused outside Emmie's door and knocked gently, suddenly filled with remorse at last night's argument over something so trivial that I'd forgotten how the whole thing had started.

I opened the door to find the room empty. A few clothes half on hangers were strewn across the unmade bed with an assortment of dangly items of jewelry dropped haphazardly in the box that doubled up as a table. There was a faint smell of cinnamon and spice in the room, undertones of the perfume she always wore.

Shutting the door carefully, I went to prepare the coffee, knowing that she would be back later on, all smiles as if nothing had happened between us. Emmie was an inborn fixer and she would have been out this morning trying to find ways of mending what had grown so fragile between us. The simple thing was, I wanted my space.

I couldn't function without it. After suffering the short fast eclipses of two marriages I'd given up looking for that perfect partner or any partner at all. It wasn't all it was cracked out to be. It was hard work and I had enough problems with myself, maintaining my mood swings enough to stay out of hospital. Bipolar disorder like most chemically based illnesses doesn't become any easier with maturity. In my case neural networks atrophy, drugs lose their efficacy and new ones have to be tried. Life was anything from living on a rollercoaster when high, to being a familiar visitor to Hades' world of shadows when I was low.

The session with Kevin was hard work, as I expected.

At 17 there is a general reluctance to therapy, mainly because it is something else imposed from the outside. Kevin answered in grunts and monosyllables. Yes, he did self-harm. He bared the inside of his forearms, revealing multiple deep scars in varying shades of red on top of earlier more refined white lines of older scars. Yes, he was on drugs, hash and alcohol only. No, he didn't have any real friends, only other drinkers and smokers. Tattoos and body jewelry seemed to adorn every piece of exposed flesh. His eyes were heavy, bloodshot from too many late nights rather than drugs and he had that aura of 'having said that. Been there. Done that...and... are you going to let me go?'

Three quarters of the way into our session I tried another approach.

"If you have an idea of what you would like in your life, right now, what would that be?"

He hesitated, his eyes sliding from mine to the door and back again and he shrugged.

"I notice you're looking at the door," I offered.

At this, his position changed: "I want out."

"Can you tell me what that looks like?"

He glared at me as if I was bonkers. "Out is out."

"Is it? Is it out of the door? Out of life?"

His eyes rested on mine again briefly, before taking a breath and letting it out slowly and, for the first time that session, I felt a connection, something at the other end of the rod I was dangling into his unconscious.

"What's that breath saying?"

"It's saying – I feel trapped and suffocated here." He pounded his chest and nonchalance gave way to anger and his eyes held mine. "Everything's shit...I just want to feel alive!"

I gave him time and space to experience the impact of his words and his feelings. I leant forwards fractionally as he glowered at me and met his troubled gaze. "What makes you feel alive, Kevin?"

He coughed nervously, stretched out his limbs and relaxed into the chair. "Fast cars, bikes...speed." He made a swishing sound at the back of his throat, "Horses racing, wolves howling…"

"Horses racing," I repeated. As in horse racing?"

"Nah," he echoed impatiently. "Horses running free…Wild horses…"

"Wild horses!" I prompted. "They're powerful animals."

"They *are* power," he said.

"Power," I repeated. "You've become really alive now. Can you feel that in your body?"

"Like a buzz!" His ankle rocked backwards and forwards.

"Yeah – like a buzz…" I amplified.

Now, here was the clinch. Our session had ended. Forty-five minutes of life and death. Between us, we had juggled implicitly with suicide…Kevin had wanted 'out'. Juxtaposed against this, life, power, and energy. These alone could either blow him away or save him with the strength of his own sense of life and power, his unlived potential.

"Kevin, I feel we're only just starting…Will you come and see me again next week?"

His features were flushed, the dark hair on his brow clinging damply against his brow. "Something had been opened up inside him just then and like Pandora's Box neither of us knew what would be revealed."

"Yeah – okay," he said.

We stood up together and I held out my hand. "I don't think you want out," I said, holding his gaze. "I think you want *in*."

I saw that he could smile for the first time, even though it was only a ghostly flutter across his lips. "Maybe."

Unlike the exhaustion I sometimes felt after a session with a new client, I felt energized. Kevin's unleashed power in the room was palpable. Throwing on a jacket, I strode out towards the park and didn't stop walking until I had gone a good mile. I sat down on a bench to watch the ducks chasing after pieces of bread thrown out across the water. My breath rose in cloudy plumes in front of me. Outside, I could feel the cold air against my skin, but inside I was on fire. It was Kevin's fire.

I walked slowly back to the house, deep in thought. Inside me, fanned a reassuring sense of knowing within me that I knew why I loved my job as a therapist. It was because I came up against people like Kevin whom others had washed their hands of, given up hope on, but for some inexplicable hugely wonderful reason revealed their true selves to me. It was because of people like Kevin who dared to face what was unbearable inside them and come up with a raw power they didn't know they had. With each client it was different.

Chapter Three

My whiskers are my dowsing rods. Because you have forgotten how to use yours, you shave them off.
Gospel of Moo

By the time I left the park, darkness was beginning to crowd the trees in sooty swathes. With the twilight, I experienced a rising nostalgia for Fly who would at this time be bounding across the park after some stick I'd thrown, racing with it back to me, whining with expectation until I seized it up and flung it into the distance again. I swallowed dryness in my throat. I did miss him terribly sometimes. I'd never been without a dog before and, given the choice between having a girlfriend or a dog, the latter would win tops. Girlfriends were complicated affairs with their emotional baggage, which tipped dangerously into my own emotional baggage.

The light was on when I arrived back. Emmie was home. And for a while I remained in the shadows, observing my life through the lens of the window, with a strange sort of detachment. I could see the flicker of the LCD television screen against the bookcase and every now and then Emmie would get up and pace the room restlessly as she probably wondered where I had got to. I knew from her behavior and body posture that she wanted to tell me something, share an exciting bit of news with me and I felt guilty about the distance that I had allowed to push up between us like a miniature forest of saplings. I could oust them out before they became too thick and unwieldy if I wanted to. But I didn't want to and this made me feel guilty. I wanted the sex with Emmie, but not the intimacy. Sex without intimacy rarely worked as I knew from experience, and already I was sabotaging the relationship.

Reluctantly, I broke free from the spell and stepped into the light of the house.

Stepped into a hallway that thrummed...

I blinked as Emmie came to greet me, her face flushed, her eyes shining as she seduced me with her smile, as if no tension had ever existed between us.

"What is it?" I asked, and then I knew as my gaze slid past the black ball of feline fluff that hurtled towards me, stopping within two inches of my feet. At first I thought it was a kitten because she was so small, but then as she steadily surveyed me, I realised she was older – much older. But it wasn't a visible thing; it was more a tangible impression. "A cat! Whose is it?"

Emmie smiled awkwardly. "I was going to break it gently...She must have slipped through the door before I shut it. I found her in town...Or rather there was a notice in the window — and I just went in and got her."

"We can't keep it," I burst out. "We have to take it back...I'm not ready for this, and a cat...I don't even *like* them."

The ball of fur mewed up at me. Except it wasn't a mew. It was; *You remember me... I spoke to you before...*

My heart seemed to stumble then race as I looked from the cat back up to Emmie incredulously. "Did you hear that?"

"What?"

"She spoke.... She actually spoke!"

Emmie shrugged. "I would've called it a 'meow' myself, but it is her way of speaking."

"She said – that she'd always known me." I sank down in the chair. "We can't keep this cat. I know nothing about cats – and..."

My words were silenced as the black ball of fur charged up my leg, tiny miniature claws snagging my jeans, until it pivoted on one knee, purring throatily.

"She likes you..."

"We'll have to take her back to the pet shop in the morning."

"She didn't come from a pet shop... I just saw a notice up in the window of a house. Here...She handed me a bright yellow piece of card."

I read, 'Special cat free to good home. No children or other animals preferred.'

"Humph…You'll just have to take her back…"

"I can't remember the address or road even, I just got lost wandering around and stumbled on it."

I grunted again and bit back a 'this is all I need!'

I awoke in the night with a sound like a motorbike throbbing in my ear and it took me a while to realize that the warmth in the curve of my neck was not Emmie's hair, but animal fur. As if sensing my wakefulness, needle claws pricked my skin painfully. The room seemed to thrum and I was aware of that strange other-worldly incandescence that I had experienced out in the Himalayas…

I've been waiting for so long…What kept you?

I fumbled for the light switch in an effort to erase this surreal dream quality from my mind. But the light only served to bring the black ball of fur into full vision against the sharp emerald brilliance of unmistakable feline eyes.

Yet, in an instant I knew that this tiny ball of fur was right. There was a deepening sense of inexplicable familiarity about her. Within her presence, I was aware of an emerging sense of something else. In psycho-synthetic terms this would be termed as the 'more than' or the transpersonal level, which could be terrifying as it was transcendental. Having lived in painful proximity to these little understood levels of consciousness, I understood their seduction and power. The fate of Icarus who flew too close to the sun with his waxen wings and plummeted back into the ocean was, in my mind, too close for comfort. And yet, there was something in human nature that yearned for the seductive glory of the transpersonal, like the 'Kevins' of the world even though the payback price was high and few who took that road ever made it back to ground level again for any length of time. Society warned about the addiction of psychedelic drugs, but it was what the drugs offered that became the real seduction. That sense of expansion, of oneness, of inner divinity and empowerment, which became a pale echo of the celestial heritage, which as Wordsworth had intimated in his work, humanity had emerged from. But as always, imprisoned by our personality, we could never really be truly free. That sense of freedom and love manifested through the Flower Power Generation came at a cost through dependence on drugs or whittling away of the personality through denial and self-discipline. Always that fine line between wanting more and more and sacrifice.

Mentally, I checked myself over with slow deliberation.

My lithium levels were okay and although the winter months could be dicey, where I tended to plummet rather than experience an emotional and mental high. At this time of the year I lived in close proximity to the underworld and Plutonian depths rather than the heights. When pomegranates appeared in supermarket aisles, I reminded myself that a descent was somewhere waiting in the wings.

And so 'Moo' as I called her, stayed and flourished, while Emmie began to fade more and more from my life until one day she wasn't there any more. She had just left with a note wishing me well. Immediately after her departure I felt a mixture of guilt and relief. Guilt because, after the Himalayan trip, we had grown further apart and I had done little to salvage what we had until nothing was left. Relief, because she had gone without a fuss or saddling me with her emotional baggage.

After three weeks, Moo had moved in with kitten bowls, an assortment of catnip toys, cat basket, scratch pole, litter tray and grooming set. After a month, I am ashamed to say, she had me firmly under her paw. She woke me up at six in the morning for her first feed, having finished off her overnight munchies. I had to sleep with the door open or she would scratch the paintwork relentlessly until I had no choice. At seven, if I were having a lie-in, she would wake me up to empty her litter tray. One of Moo's steaming 'poos' was guaranteed to get me out of bed fast. I had to give her full reign of the house or she would start plucking at my trousers. This plucking could go on for anything up to an hour, so that every pair of trousers I had consisted of pluck marks. The cat bed I had bought was made redundant from the first day as Moo insisted on sleeping on my bed, usually managing to burrow underneath the covers where her claws would make their presence known if I slept for too long or too deeply.

I don't know whether I was a natural 'cat whisperer' as up until Moo arrived in my life, I had had nothing to do with cats. But I understood most of what she was saying. I say 'most' because sometimes there were things she said, especially when she was impatient or irritable, that she didn't want me to understand. She would tell me what sort of a day she'd had which consisted of how much attention I had given her, whether I had given her treats and the quality of the weather. Like all cats, she hated rain, where she would go regularly through the performance of insisting being let out another door or window in the belief that the weather might be better there. Knowing she was an intelligent enough creature to work this out for herself; that different doors didn't open out onto different worlds, I knew maintenance of this belief consisted of vast levels of denial. The sort of denial that is embedded in human nature when it comes to romantic relationships, and the effect of alcohol and nicotine. She wasn't keen on dogs and stared at them disdainfully as she did with me sometimes.

Six months into our relationship, I noticed Moo was taking a keen interest in the assortment of clients visiting me. Like most cats I had heard about, she took a peculiar shine to clients who ignored her or didn't like her.

Moo hated being ignored and above being liked, needed to be respected. That's why Moo understood the Unconditional Positive Regard part of therapy. This was based on Rogerian counseling created by American psychologist, Carl Rogers, who believed that the client had everything within them to achieve wholeness. But this healing process may have been submerged through faulty environmental conditioning early in the biographical history. By utilizing the three main tools of Humanistic Counseling which were *empathy, congruence* and *respect,* this faulty behavior could be corrected. Unlike Freud, whose work on the unconscious formed the bedrock of most analyses and therapy, Rogerian therapy concentrated on mirroring back to the client the qualities he didn't know he had rather than the defects he knew only too well were present.

Because my therapy practice took place inside my home, I had worked hard to establish strong boundaries between my personal life and what went on inside the therapy room. These divisions held up for as long as Moo hadn't been around. Little by little, as client after client walked through my doors, Moo gradually began to erode those boundaries I had struggled so hard to erect.

Moo was particularly fond of Kevin, who visited me for eighteen months. And he was fond of her, although he never mentioned anything about understanding her language. She would be sitting waiting for him to arrive by the door. Even if he accidentally came on the wrong day or the wrong time, she would be waiting for him. At first, I had been stunned by her ability to intuit his arrival when I didn't know myself, but then I took it for granted. There were a lot of things about Moo that could not be accounted for. Whenever I asked her how she knew, or questioned her infallible ability to know when someone was coming or something was going to happen, she would blank me as if I had insulted her, which I probably had. When Moo blanked me, she refused to speak 'my language' as she called it and sat with her back to me. If it went on too long which it had been known to over several days, I found it painful and begged her forgiveness. I had never had to beg anyone for anything before, least of all a cat.

Chapter Four

In the beginning was fur. And fur was good. God has fur.
Gospel according to Moo

Communicating with Moo became one of the most natural things to do in the world.

Correction! As Moo said, true communicating wasn't doing, it was *being*. No action was involved except a willingness to open up and be receptive. Although Moo meowed as all cats do, her communication of intention and information took place in the silence. And it was a two-way thing. As she thought to me, I thought back to her.

One of our ongoing dialogues was about fur, or the lack of it.

Moo believed that the fundamental root of human problems was simply being without fur. Being furless, at the very least, made people grumpy and lonely. At the most, it made people greedy, jealous and desperate. Fur wasn't just about keeping warm. It was about the fear of being naked or seen naked. This wasn't, Moo explained, just a physical nakedness, but an existential one of never truly feeling at home, safe or cared for in the world. That was why humans needed psychotherapists and counselors like animals and myself.

Really people needed to see fur therapists, like Moo.

The dark side of this furless state of being was that people became so preoccupied with their lack, that they wasted their whole lives in the pursuit of fur substitutes in the form of clothes and maintenance of the tiny bit of fur they did have on their head. And as with any existential deficit, no one was ever happy with the fur they did have. They would cut it off, grow it in exasperation, color and bleach it and cover it up with an assortment of scarves and hats. Even worse, they would shave it off and that included whiskers. Moo really couldn't see the sanity in shaving off whiskers, for men or older women, because they were nature's natural dowsing rods; offering up information on whether other humans were safe to be around, if the weather was going to change or whether danger was skulking about in the wings somewhere. And if men did have whiskers or beards, they had forgotten how to use them and learned to disregard the impulses emanating from one's interior and exterior world.

Even darker still, was the inherent and growing preoccupation with fur and accessing it through cruel and despicable means. Moo believed that stealing and killing another for their fur was the worst kind of sin, especially as people no longer needed it to survive. By doing this or paying into the mindless slaughter that amassing huge amounts of fur created, humans set up a karmic backlog with the animal kingdom. This, in short, was why humans would suffer from guilt and shame about this act, which in turn gave rise to deep and unremitting depression. Most depression, she believed was about the loss and pursuit of fur.

Moo surprised me in being such a firm believer in the virtues of technology. She loved anything technological and insisted on spending hours draped across my computer screen. I had one of those old fashioned models with a huge monitor that thrummed with warmth and Moo even remarked that she loved it because it purred. It seemed that we had created machines that purred and spoke her language better than we did. I gave up worrying whether the computer would overheat or even blow up after I realized that there was nothing I could do to stop her. If I closed the door when I was working on it, she would mew endlessly, and even if I wore my headphones to block her out, I knew she was pluck, plucking at the carpet, systematically shredding the fibers as well as my nerves. Most of the time I would forget she was there until she draped her tail over the screen, so I had to carefully put it back, or peer round it to see what I was doing. If her tail was resistant and kept coming back to the screen, I knew there was something she was trying to communicate and I had to stop what I was doing to give her my full attention. She did this with the television screen too. Moo was an avid and insatiable television viewer. Not only because it was warm and 'purred', she also liked what was on it, especially the wildlife programs. But, most of all, she loved snooker, which wasn't a problem as I liked it too. However, she did have an annoying habit of going right up to the screen to watch intently, while the player deliberated with his cue and then her paw, fast as lightning would pounce on the ball as it shot across the snooker table. Once I'd got a busy evening with clients and set the video player to record one of my favorite thrillers, *Trial and Retribution*. Looking for it the next day, part of the program had vanished off into snooker. Moo ever drawn by any mechanical whirring or clicking sound and anything that flashed had pressed buttons she shouldn't have and, as a result, come out with a recording of her favorite program.

We never communicated about things like that. She would look at me with that innocent 'who me?' expression when I glowered at her.

Several times, I remember thinking how human she was. Reading my thoughts she said: *Maybe it's because I am human.*

"What are you doing in a cat's body then, Moo, if you're human?" I countered.

She slowly licked her paw before answering and I thought at first I hadn't got my message across, but her ears were back, listening, waiting for the right moment. Moo knew how to bide her time, how to increase the tension of needing to have an answer. After she had completed washing her paw she carefully put it down again and looked directly at me.

I was human once...

"When?"

Many years ago in the time of one of your first civilizations. She looked at me, reading my thoughts. *Yes, it was in Egypt...I was a pharaoh's child and I had a cat of my own...That was when they were sacred and valued because they were truly seen and heard...*

"Which pharaoh?"

Moo sighed. *Does it matter?*

"Yes."

If I tell you...You'll become all caught up in details and will lose what I am trying to communicate to you. She was right. Moo's life as a child would be completely overshadowed by the historical glory of knowing an ex-pharaoh's child firsthand.

"You said you were a child?"

Yes...I had a happy childhood...But then I died.

"How?"

A scorpion. I was bitten by a scorpion...If I'd had thick fur I don't think it would have happened.

"I suppose you're talking about reincarnation? Did you come back as a human again?"

No.

"Why ever not? You were happy as a child, weren't you?"

Yes, but being naked was terrifying...I decided not to.

"Did you have a choice?"

Moo deliberated and washed her other paw. *Yes...*

"But, from what I remember about the theory of reincarnation, it's progressive rather than regressive. Even if you believe in the Hindu belief of transmigration, you will have had to do something really bad to regress from human form into animal form...From what I understand Moo, if you remain as an animal, you won't progress any more." I stopped, noticing Moo's tail beginning to swish.

I was picking up something that I had never experienced in her before, defensiveness. Of course defensiveness was something I encountered frequently in my work with clients when they felt I was challenging strong mindsets.

I don't want to progress any more.

"But – you're so human as it is..."

Moo's tailed resumed its fury.

"Why Moo?"

She turned slowly back to me and made a thing of rubbing her face with her paw without licking it first. *It terrifies me to live a life without fur…I might forget..*

"Forget what?"

What it's like **with** *fur,* Moo replied soberly. *I might go to sleep and become unconscious."*

Her inner turmoil was tangible.

"But Moo," I countered excitedly, experiencing that same sense of breakthrough as I did with one of my clients. "Isn't it painful to be conscious…To know, but not be able to act or express…To become mute in a cat body…"

The rest of my words trailed off as Moo jumped down from the windowsill and pulled the door open with her paw. Moo was disturbed and angry and behaving exactly like one of my clients who were about to have a breakthrough.

After that, Moo refused to communicate with me for three whole weeks. To me, this was nothing short of interminable. And Moo knew it. I lost count of the times I begged and cajoled her to be in a dialogue with me again. She just made the perfunctory sounds that any cat made for food, water and to pass in and out of doors, but that was all. If we were in the same room, she sat with her back to me, ears stationed on neutral. She stopped jumping up on my bed and insisted on staying out most of the night. I didn't know that being exiled by a cat could be so painful that it was humiliating. I had become dependent on her for comfort and support. In fact her rejection had me going through morbid reflective exercises. Why couldn't I hold down relationships with others? When my last relationship with Emmie was breaking down, instead of rescuing it, I let it go. Now, I couldn't even sustain a relationship with a cat…And yet, had I imagined that I had experienced a relationship with her. Wasn't she just an ordinary everyday moggy that I was projecting all my deeply repressed longings for the transpersonal on? Even worse, I thought as the rain streaked down the window panes, maybe by imagining that I was in communication with Moo, was a symptom that I was cycling between the emotional extremes. Perhaps, I wasn't as well as I thought I was and my dialogue with Moo was a symptom of my illness.

Just when I couldn't bear it anymore, Moo came back to me.

One morning I felt her padding gently up my duvet and held my breath as she came up to my face and licked my chin.

What did Emmie give you? She trilled softly.

"You, of course."

There was a soft approving purr at my answer and the morbid thoughts left me. *The sun's shining,* she announced, *and you need to get up.*

"Oh Moo," I murmured, reaching for her. "You've come back…"

Moo had launched herself at the suit hanging on the door and I didn't even wince as she plucked at the expensive fiber with those claws of hers. The room buzzed. I heard her running round the house and diving out through the cat flap I had put in, then diving back in again and onto my bed.

Spring, she trilled. *Come on – get up…Kevin's coming today.*

"No, he's not."

Yes, he is!

I knew better than to argue with Moo. She had dowsed it with her whiskers. The most important thing was Moo was back. And it was Spring!

Chapter Five

Humans are very clumsy with their wireless connections. Cats are wireless too but their whiskers are a lot neater.
Gospel of Moo

Moo was right of course.

About the time she had sauntered up the garden path to sit up on the wall, Kevin swept round the corner on his bike. Within the eighteen months he had been coming to me each week, he had transformed from an angry, depressed young man, desperately trapped inside a body that he found hard to fit, to a calmer self-assured person who had a life of his own. A few days before his eighteenth birthday, he had moved away from his family to a bed-sit, half a mile away. The area wasn't as rough and nearer his college. Knowing all the pre-personal junk such life changing moves could unearth in a young person, I watched over him like the father he had never had. But all my concern about his being able to adapt to the new move was unfounded. He didn't fall back into drug taking or drinking alcohol. He literally seemed to fill out in worldly and bodily stature and take up his place in the world. It was incredible to witness and I was proud of him and proud of myself for investing all the unpaid extra time I had in him. He was living evidence of how psychotherapy worked and could sustain a client.

I watched him stop to stroke Moo as she reared up on her hind legs to meet his hand. Moo was as flirtatious as she was clever. She rarely had anything to do with my female clients and sometimes sulked if they stayed over their hour, even though I tried to explain that running overtime was inevitable if a natural closure couldn't be found. She never minded Kevin staying overtime and always knew when the phone rang if it was him. At first Kevin had been indifferent to her, but over time Moo charmed him as she did everyone.

I could see Kevin looked well. A couple of months ago he had started dating a girl at the college and even brought her along to meet me. He had passed his mock A-levels and if he did as well in his real ones, he stood a good chance of getting into University. He had deliberated between being a vet or a wildlife photographer, as he could then travel more and be a part of a world that was growing and changing fast.

But I was also aware of the history he had emerged from. One that included a father in prison for manslaughter and a mother who suffered from episodes of schizophrenic psychosis; when she would be hospitalized for weeks at a time. His younger brothers and sister were feral by nature and he had little to do with them since leaving home, because they occupied a twilight world of drugs and dealing. It was a world that he had fought hard to stay away from. I knew that when change entered his life, it would bring up old wounds and insecurities around the past and the future. In an ideal society young people going into the world would have supportive parents that they knew they could depend on if things were rocky in the beginning. In this respect, new beginnings could be anticipated with nervous excitement rather than fearful apprehension. For the young unsupported adults in their formative years each new challenge was full of black holes and terrifying chasms lurking beneath the surface. Self-awareness and consciousness around one's weakness could only help to a degree; the rest was sheer willpower and determination. In Kevin's case, I just hoped that our eighteen months working together in therapy would build a good sound foundation that would hold strong. Compounding the structural difficulties in his early background were stronger genetic ones overriding this. He had inherited some of his mother's psychotic nature as well as his father's raw anger. He knew this and, as a result, exercised some autonomy over otherwise instinctual driven actions. But it wasn't easy. And it must have been tempting to become one of those countless individuals emerging from similar backgrounds who preferred to think that the world was happening to them rather than realizing their personal autonomy through the choices they made.

Kevin followed me into the room, sat down as he usually did, right leg crooked over his left thigh. Head cocked on one side, studying me, waiting for a prompt.

"How's it going?" I asked.

"Oh fine," he offered. "I'm still happy in the bed-sit...I love having my own space and that..."

I waited a few moments allowing the sense of Kevin's newfound space to flow in, taking up the room. It felt warm and inviting, something Kevin had earned.

"And Jill?"

"Yeah," he rocked his foot, "She's fine..." He grinned at me. "She's good...We're good..."

The silence again and I waited, deliberately keeping myself in the background. I was still amazed at how eager my words were to make themselves known, to steer the session into more superficial areas where speech came easily.

Silence was hard for both client and therapist, although a good therapist knew the value of silence and what could be held in the deepening and widening space. Silence gave an opportunity for what was hidden, tamped down, to find a voice.

"What about college and your work there?"

Kevin shrugged and he changed his position, stuck his legs out in front of him as if pushing me away. "It's okay.... I'm doing okay."

There was a fine prickling of something more held in the silence. Something held in captivity.

"How do you want to spend this session?"

He shrugged, changed his position again. "I dunno, really."

"Have you thought about which university you'd like to go

to?" I tried.

"Yeah...Possibly Loughborough or Lancaster."

"That far away?"

"Well, they do the courses I want to do…"

"Manchester's good, isn't it?"

"Yeah. I just want to make a new start."

Again the prickling, the undercurrent I couldn't quite name.

"You want to make a new start," I repeated slowly.

"What's wrong with that?" he swung back defensively.

"Nothing really." I paused fractionally. "Except I know that beginnings are difficult for you…That going to Loughborough will take you a long way from home."

"Home! Huh… I have no home."

I was surprised at the bitterness in his voice. I hadn't heard that for a few months.

"You have Jill…"

"Who wants to settle down," he broke in savagely, "and probably have a baby. I'm not ready for that yet."

He scowled at the wall.

"So you're running away."

Anger darkened his features and then I saw him breathe into his belly, as I had taught him to do…"I'm just starting a new life."

"Away from Jill?"

He looked down; studying his hands as if they belonged to someone else and then his shoulders slouched forward. "It's not as if she's said she wants to settle down but she wants to move in with me."

Still, the fine prickling and, on almost a subliminal level, I sensed a warning sign in the form of a little red door that was swinging open at the back of my mind. Almost unconsciously I reached for the door to peer into the darkness that hung at the edges, but in a flash it had slammed shut and been obliterated. I waited a few moments. "Having a partner move in is a major event. I can understand why you feel as you do."

He relaxed a little. "If she moves in…It's only a small flat, she'll take over and I'll feel squashed out."

"I can understand that…But does it have to be so drastic?"

He shrugged. "What else?"

"Well, you could wait a bit…Has she mentioned wanting a family?"

"Nah."

"Have you asked her?"

"Nah."

"Do you love her?"

He winced. "No…I don't know…Yes, perhaps I do."

I drew back, glanced at the clock and saw we had a few minutes left before the end of the session, but also observed we were standing on important ground. Ground that was too fragile to hurry through, or to reach a closure. But, still I ended the session there with the ground between us, giving him time to think about what he wanted, what he was afraid of. For a while I sat in the silence. Holding the space, Kevin's space and feeling very drained and exhausted as if I had done a work-out at the gym.

The space is very often the work of the counselor. Space between sessions, between the client and myself and the space left in the therapy room that holds all the things that are unconscious and the things that might have been said but haven't been said. Things that close in, and wait around until the next session.

There are a lot of myths about counseling and therapy; one is that we make a lot of money from doing nothing. This isn't true. Deep and life changing work goes on in the therapy room. And, in many ways, the silence is more important than the words.

In the silence is a deep sense of listening. You see, listening isn't a passive thing; it's both active and dynamic. In actuality, it is very hard to listen. As a modern culture our listening skills are zilch. Anybody who doesn't agree with this should try it. Try listening. It's not just a matter of sitting listening with a clenched jaw until someone has finished so that you can have your say. It is about opening up, dropping down into the centre of yourself and suspending judgment. Taking judgment out of the equation is the hardest thing to do and yet...Listening without judgment automatically takes one to deeper levels of being.

It's a bit like sitting by the sea or beside a river. At first there is the sound of the overriding currents or waves, which seems to drown all else. But listening deeper you drop down beneath the sound, and become aware of finer subterranean nuances nudging beneath that threshold of awareness. It's akin to listening to the whole person, rather than the part that wants to be heard.

However genuine your intention, the mind does tend to slip away, like a kite restlessly wanting to escape its moorings and dare the next adventure. You become aware of your own personal voice, the judgment creeping in and you hear yourself think... "Oh, this is so boring...We've been here before so many times." Or your tummy rumbles and you realize you haven't had anything to eat since breakfast. The phone rings in the next room and even though you know the answer phone will kick in, you can't help wondering who it is – whether it's the garage ringing to say your car is ready.

Believe me, it takes energy to listen, to really listen. Because, on one level, you're listening to the content of the conversation, and where the energy is being taken. But on another, you're also listening for those subtle undercurrents, listening for what is still held in the silence. Some of this is held in the body, so you look for that too. Listening for what is being held in the body is quite easy once you get used to it. If you assume that most of our communications are about saying what the other person wants or expects to hear, rather than what you really think or feel, then you will understand what is held in the feet, hands and buttocks.

Moo knows how to listen in this way. She listens with all of her being including her whiskers and tail. She will listen to the thoughts before they drop into words and respond to them. She is an opportunist because she will find the empty spaces in a person's mind and slot in images of tuna fish, which is her favourite, and coley. I used to think that it was I who was intuitive and reading her mind, but she later told me that she had planted them in my mind. She explained to me once that it was important to have spaces in your mind to allow things in, like new thoughts. Space allowed new ideas to germinate. When she went on about this, I worried that I had too much blank space in my mind and that most of the thoughts I had were not my own. She agreed that most of the thoughts in my mind were not my own invention, but collective ones that were swimming around waiting for an empty space to fall into. Empty space, Moo maintained, was good because it had the potential to be productive. She said most people's minds were so full of junk that there was no space for a whisker to grow or a thought to germinate, let alone a tin of tuna. This junk was made of intellectual and emotional mindsets that kept the owner slave to themselves. She maintained that many humans seemed to be so afraid of space and the unknown that they filled their minds with incessant activity that made them compulsive and gave rise to addictive behaviors. I had to agree with her and at times like this I wondered and fretted about the future of the human race.

Chapter Six

When you feel you have lost something, reach into the hole it has left in order to find the gift.... If you can't find the gift, you may have to lose something else to find it...
Gospel of Moo

Pluck, pluckety pluck...Plucker-doodledoo!

It seemed like only five minutes after falling asleep, I was being jerked awake by sharp needles puncturing my neck and stabbing my face. Muttering, I turned and changed my position in the bed, every cell in my body wanting to sink back into the oblivion I had emerged from.

Pluck...Pluck...Pluck...

But those needles were relentless and I sat up abruptly, throwing both Moo and duvet off my bed. "What the hell is it, Moo?" I grumbled.

Kevin...It's Kevin, came her urgent response. *He needs your help.*

Jerking on the light, I stared at her. "What?"

You have to get to him...Or else it'll be too late.

I blinked, aware that my heart was drumming in panic because in that instant I knew that she was right. Kevin did need help. I reached for my glasses and car keys simultaneously before pulling on trainers T-shirt and jeans. And then I stopped. "I don't know his address...The number..."

17 Macclesfield Road... Moo dropped into my thoughts.

Momentarily, I checked myself as a saner part of myself surfaced; what the heck was I doing? Had I completely flipped? Taking orders from a cat to visit a client of mine who was, seemingly, in dire straits. This was the middle of the night. Three in the morning! I was already going against all that I had been taught about honoring my client's privacy, autonomy and integrity. He hadn't even contacted me for help.

Yet, he had…I could confirm this as fragments of the dream Moo roused me from came sliding back into place to form an identical picture. In the dream Kevin was talking to me; telling me all the things that he had held back from the therapy session. In the dream, he had spoken of his fear of 'going into the world', becoming a fully-fledged adult, going to university and leaving everything he had known and held familiar behind. It was one of those treacly dreams where you had to work very hard to exert any impact on the events you were caught up in. Each time I reached out to Kevin, he withdrew from me, becoming amorphous. Moo was only echoing my own fears.

Feebly, before leaving the house, I tried his number and then gave up as the answer phone clicked in. I wanted to go back to bed and drop, this time, into the welcome pool of oblivion.

Moo was getting agitated; pluck, plucking at my trouser leg. *Hurry*, she urged.

I did hurry…I rang the ambulance, explaining that I had a tip-off about one of my clients who was dangerously depressed and would they go round to his home and check…They did and I went round to Kevin's myself, in time to see the blue light of the ambulance flashing; the stretcher being carried out and I followed them to the hospital. "Are you a relative?" someone had asked.

"No, therapist. I'm his therapist," I responded automatically.

"Do you know how we can contact his parents? "

I scribbled down Kevin's surname and repeated details that he had shared in confidence about his mother's whereabouts on the Moss Side Estate. It wouldn't take the police long to track his Mum down.

By the time I got back home it was five in the morning and I suddenly felt drained and exhausted. Unplugging the land phone, I slipped back into bed without disturbing Moo who was sleeping peacefully at the end of it. I had a new client at two o'clock this afternoon and was reluctant to cancel this as my financial resources had been low lately and I needed the money. There was nothing more I could do for Kevin now. He was in the hands of the experts. I just wanted to sink into a dreamless sleep and let all the guilt and anxieties wash away. Guilt, because I had breached a client's confidence, broken that verbal contract of confidentiality whether it was for his ultimate good or not.

I slept, but it was a troubled one, full of violent flashbacks from my own past; as a child running away from a lecherous uncle who seemed to always want to see me undressed so that he could take pictures and touch me. The same uncle that I had found hanging from the stairwell, a dark stain of pee on the carpet below, eyes open and staring down at me, pupils black and huge. At his suicide, all I had experienced was a deep sense of relief; that I could breathe into myself again because my life was no longer a dirty secret hidden from everyone but me. He had been a depressive like his brother, my father. And all these years I had nursed a secret fear that I was a covert pedophile; that because I suffered from depression, I was tainted by the same perverse genetic lineage as my uncle. Entering into the therapy training had opened up this deep wound of shame and slowly the pus had leaked out until the wound was purged and ran clear. But the wound was always there and somehow Kevin's suicide attempt had triggered off a relapse into painful shadowy memories.

I woke, drenched in cold sweat to the urgent shrill of the alarm in my ear. My first thought when I looked at the clock and saw that I only had an hour until my new client arrived, was of Kevin. There was a sinking feeling deep in the pit of my stomach, which came from a sense of failure. I had failed him. I should have known that he was on the edge of crisis. I should have picked it up. I remembered the red door of warning that had opened in my mind during our last session. Remembered how, reaching for it, it had slammed shut again. Red was for danger. I should have read the symptom.

Stop punishing yourself! Moo purred into my thoughts.

I relaxed a little as she walked up the duvet to my face. *It's not your fault*

"I feel it is, Moo..."

I know you do...But it's his journey...The important thing is that he'll survive this... Her whiskers brushed, comfortingly, against my chin.

I stared at her groggily. "Will he?" I thought back. "I've breached the therapeutic contract with him."

Moo purred more deeply. Once I had found this purring in the midst of trauma and turmoil deeply irritating, until Moo had explained that it was a cat's way of soothing whatever was in distress as she would her own kittens.

Of course... He'll be in a hospital a couple of days, then go to another place which will help his mind.

"You mean psychiatric care?"

Yes...What's wrong with that? It'll be good for him.

"In what way can it be good for him?" I challenged.

Moo looked down at me and I sensed a smile as if it came from her soul.

In the same way that it was good for you, she responded gently. *Your life changed after that, remember?*

I had to agree. Unlike Kevin I had managed to stay away from hospitalization until I was twenty-two. That was amidst my first full-blown manic episode where I had been caught on the rooftop of my University waiting for a UFO to take me away to a saner planet. I had the right intuition, but it required implementation on a saner level than I was on. I was euphoric as the flashing lights of the police vehicles buzzed distantly below, but I was also partly mesmerized by the shiny red fire engine arching its ladder up towards me. A crowd gathered below and I experienced omnipotence at the fact that I was the main attraction...I had the message from 'them above' to transform the environment, the country, and the world.

Wisely, my rescuers played along with me while they called out a psychiatrist to section me and I was chaperoned off to the 'funny farm' with a skinful of haloperidol. There I slowly came to within a locked, secure ward. And as I fell down to a more sane level, I received my diagnosis and slowly all the quirky things about my life, characterized by my moods, made sense. Having a diagnosis was a relief. I stayed for several weeks in hospital where I learned all about my condition and how medications such as mood stabilizers were absolutely vital to my well-being. In my secure quarter, I met one of my ex-science tutors who had been 'off sick' for several months, a nurse who thought she was the divine incarnation of Florence Nightingale and Razor who got his name from the numerous scars criss-crossing his torso and arms. We were all 'locked up' mainly for our own safety, but also, I felt, for everyone else's safety too.

After three months inside, I had taken a year out from Uni to get used to the real sane world again and receive therapy which helped, but didn't take away my diagnosis or rescue me from the cycles of emotional instability I was subject too. What I did understand was that I had a serious life-threatening illness that was never really going to go away. Much later, I learned that this was the wound that all good therapists, doctors and healthcare professionals healed through. My number one rule was to know that medication was a way of life. Without it, I would go under – and never come up again.

"You're right Moo," I agreed. But – how did you know about Kevin? When did you know? Did you know yesterday afternoon?"

Moo licked her paw. *I knew something was wrong…I sensed it in my whiskers, like a trembling.*

"Why didn't you say anything to me?"

You told me never to interfere with your therapy sessions, Moo thought back swiftly.

"I know…But this was life-threatening."

So, I told you…I let you know…

"It could have been too late though."

Stop blaming me for something you're blaming yourself for not picking up on.

"I'm sorry… You're right, of course."

He will be okay…It's part of his journey.

"Moo – I want you to promise that if you foresee something like this again to let me know."

But it's interfering with your autonomy.

"I know," I tickled her behind her ears. "Sometimes though, you have to interfere with that…As I might have to interfere with yours…"

Moo's purr deepened as she surrendered to the scratching. *It can be difficult for me too.*

I stopped "What can?"

Interfering with your free will.

"In what way, Moo?"

"It affects your evolution and mine."

I didn't have time to pursue the subject further because I could see that I only had half an hour before my new client came. Having only minutes to spritz around the house, make myself presentable, and feed Moo got me out of bed faster than I thought I was capable of.

Tina, my new client was a large, or rather a morbidly obese Asian woman of about 30 whose presenting problem was overeating and a punishing regime of working up to sixteen hours a day. Her eating was not only her means of dealing with stress in the media communications company she owned and ran, it was also her way of deflecting intimacy. In her words: "I make myself big so that people can't get near me."

The deflection of intimacy and workaholic temperament was her way of subjugating painful memories that seemed to rise up like a geyser whenever she stopped or tried to enjoy herself. She was, as I thought, a victim of child abuse. Raped at fourteen by a cousin, she had kept this as a dark secret from her family, especially as the person who raped her was a favored family member.

"How do you find your enjoyment?" I asked, "apart from eating and working?"

"I hate eating and working, "she corrected. "I hate what it does to me...I can honestly say, I don't know what enjoyment is." She spread surprisingly small delicate hands, "but it must be better than working every hour I'm awake and consuming everything like a black hole."

Black hole, I thought, *fear of annihilation?* That was a biggie in victims of abuse. I deliberated in challenging her about this head on, shelving processing until a later occasion. Not that Tina was fragile, but it was too early in the relationship.

"What does eating and working all these hours do for you?" I asked instead.

"It anaesthetizes me. But..."

"But?"

She turned to me, "I want to *feel* again without being tortured by those same feelings. I've had a number of therapists and psychiatrists in my life. I've tried the spiritual, new age path of past life regressions which helped at the time, but haven't cured me...I chose you because you have a psychological background and the type of therapy you use embraces the spiritual."

I liked her clarity of purpose and vision.

"What do you want out of this therapy?"

There was a long silence. The silence that held deep unresolved issues, potential that hadn't been tapped, deep fears about the known and the unknown.

"Well money and status hasn't made me happy as society promises...I just want a sense of peace..." She let her breath out in a controlled way so that it whistled through the gap in her front teeth.

"Peace." I echoed slowly. I spread my hands questioningly, "What would this peace look like?"

Again the silence and I felt myself begin to breathe more deeply. This deepening was so important and it took courage to tolerate it in a world that demanded instant results and movement. I noticed she had closed her eyes without my even asking her. A pulse in her neck throbbed rapidly; her hands trembled, belying any sense that she was relaxing.

"Peace... would be..."

I waited for a few minutes after her voice trailed off and ventured slowly. "Peace can be..."

I saw the film of perspiration on her brow and had a fleeting sense of fear that we were moving too fast for a first session. And yet, it wasn't I that was moving. She had her hands on the control button and I sensed the depth of her need to move onto the next stage of her life. More time passed and I had an image of her dropping down and down, away from me. I too began to sweat as if I was bearing her physical weight as she dropped down and down.

I threw her a lifeline. "How are you feeling now? Where are you, Tina?"

A voice a long way away, small childlike, "I'm holding a red balloon and...I can feel the breeze...."

"You're holding a red balloon," I amplified, "and you can feel the breeze..."

"Yes," her voice became stronger and more excited, "I can taste the breeze..."

"What does it taste of?"

"Salt," came the decisive response.

"Where are you, Tina? Can you see where you are?"

"I'm on the beach...I can hear the gulls. They're swooping down to the waves..."

"You're on the beach...How do you feel, Tina? What are you experiencing?"

Nothing at first. Then a childish giggle. "I'm feeling peaceful...so very peaceful..."

I felt myself breathe again, experiencing her sense of peace and relief that, although she had regressed to another time and place in her life, she was still in dialogue with me. I sensed her strength, the strength that she had galvanized into securing her goals in the world as well as the self-created wall of flesh around her to keep out intruders.

"Is there anyone with you?" I asked.

"No," came the swift answer. "I'm on my own, and I'm peaceful."

"That's good. Tina...Now I want you to come slowly back, knowing that this peace you experience is there within you whenever you need it.

A little child's voice: "I don't want to come back..."

"You have to," I said. "It's important...But this place that you've found on the beach with the gulls will always be here for you..."

"I want to bring back the red balloon."

"Go on then..."

By the time Tina was finally herself, in the therapy room, I realized forty-five minutes had passed. I swiftly brought the session to a close. "We've covered a lot in one session, Tina...Especially as it's our first...How are you feeling now?"

She flashed large even white teeth, "Good, I actually feel good!"

"Can we make an appointment for next week?"

She grinned. "Too right," she agreed.

We made a date and after she had gone I was aware of a sense of exhaustion. Therapy was exhausting. But it had gone well for a first session. If it had been anyone else, I would have been worried about the swift descent into a meditative state. But Tina was what we termed in therapy, 'a sophisticated client'. Someone who wasn't new to therapy and for this reason had already done a lot of psychological and reparative work on themselves. Again, I was amazed at how, during the therapy space when there was a real connection with the client, all outside problems dropped away.

Remembering Kevin, I rang the hospital. They immediately demanded to know if I was a relative. They were cagey when I said I was a therapist, but were able to confirm that his condition was stable and that tomorrow he was moving from High Dependency onto Ward Nine, a normal medical ward.

I would go in to visit him tomorrow evening. He needed all the support he could get.

Chapter Seven

Everyone sees God in their own image...God has fur.
Gospel of Moo

But that time didn't come.

Kevin refused to see me and broke off all contact. Despite all my training and experience of distressed and disturbed patients, I still felt gutted. Kevin had been almost like a son to me. Unprofessionally, I hung onto the memory that Moo had predicted this happening, and had brushed it aside; assuring me it was only a temporary cessation in our relationship. But when it came down to it, who could I trust? A cat or Kevin? In the cold light of this reality, there seemed to be no contest...

The only time I allowed Moo in the therapy room was when Kirsten, a seventeen- year-old demanded it. She was a mixed up kid whom my old friend, Michelle, had referred to me. "I don't know quite what her problem is," Michelle wheezed over the phone. "She's on medication for depression and psychosis, but she desperately needs a good session of therapy. She's been through a number of psychologists who have all given up on her." She broke off to give way to another bout of coughing.

"You sound awful, you should take time off work and get that throat better."

"I know...." Michelle croaked, "but, we both know 'm my own worst enemy. The root of it is smoking, as you know. Anyway, I'm pushed for time just now...I'll fax you the rest."

"Is she up for therapy though?" I pressed. "You know not everyone can take to it..."

"I think she's an ideal candidate because she has a passion for..." more coughing.

"For what?"

"Animals!"

"Animals…I think she believes they had something to do with her upbringing. It might be a bit of False Memory Syndrome. But she seems to think she'd developed a very special relationship with an Alsatian. Look…" she spluttered. "I have to go out and make a home visit. I'm already late. Kirsten…Will you take her?"

I vacillated, but only briefly, and then took on my new client. I needed to build up my clientele. February was a difficult time for me. It was easy to feel myself sinking at this time of the year. There was a lot to be said for keeping busy as a defense against consciousness. The difference here was that I, at least, was conscious of my need to keep busy in order to keep depressive descent at bay. And besides, this new case sounded interesting.

Moo, not usually that partial to the female sex, seemed to take Kirsten under her paw. And it was good to see the two of them together. Moo was invited into the therapy room during Kirsten's second visit, when the poor girl had her arms wrapped around herself and was rocking backwards and forwards. The soft toys that I had for my clients were tersely rejected. Worse…hurled across the room!

"Fur…" Kirsten continued rocking backwards and forwards, "I want fur!"

In exasperation I had opened the door and Moo, waiting directly outside, moved easily across the room and jumped right up onto the girl's lap, nudging her hand, licking the tears from her fingers, purring throughout.

I watched as Kirsten's breathing slowed and she visibly relaxed into Moo's presence. Moo settled her small relaxed form along the length of Kirtsen's arm, eyes half closed, looking back at me and smiling. Before Moo, I would have laughed if anyone had said that animals smile, but they do. Maybe Lewis Carroll had it right, after all, when he included the Grinning Cheshire Cat in his fabled Wonderland. Moo could grin too.

"I feel so much better now," Kirsten admitted at length. "Can I come again?"

"Of course you can...But I think it's a cat you need more than me, or fur as you say...Can't you have animals at home?"

Kirsten shook her head. "Mum suffers from asthma and she's allergic to cats and dogs, well...Fur."

"What does fur give you?" I asked.

Kirsten wiped away her stray tears with the cuff of her sweat-shirt. "Fur gives me a sense of home, of belonging."

"What does the sense of belonging and fur look like.."

Kirsten giggled.

"What's funny?"

"Did you know your cat talks?"

I flushed a little with embarrassment as Moo looked back at me with that told-you-so, expression of hers.

"What is she saying?"

She giggled again.

"She says you're asking silly questions...And that if you had listened properly, I had already told you that fur was home and gave me a sense of belonging..."

Part of me wanted to agree with her, especially about Moo being a talking cat and what she said was perfectly true. But this was a professional relationship, and it was important for everyone that we kept it that way. I was concerned that, inadvertently, Kirsten might leak news to her Mum about her 'mad' therapist who could understand what animals said. 'Animal whisperer therapist' emblazoned across the local newspaper would be the end of my career.

"Do you often talk to animals?" I asked, still aware of my cheeks burning as Moo continued to look at me with that classic, irritatingly superior look that all cats seemed to have.

"No," Kirsten responded. "They talk to me first."

When I agreed to take Kirsten on, I hadn't really been prepared for what I was letting myself in for. In any other client, or if it hadn't been for my dialogue with Moo, I would have expected strong issues of projection in the counter-transference, yet I only picked up a genuine congruence in the space between us. But, as I let Kirsten out the front door, I couldn't help intuiting a strong sense of being outnumbered, and Moo having one over on me.

Somehow that sense of being put down, however harmless the intent, gave me the courage to approach Moo again on the subject of evolution. Since she had mentioned it the other day in connection with Kevin's attempted suicide, I hadn't been able to let it go. My fear was that she would blank me out as she had last time, or even leave. My hope was that I would learn a little more about Moo. As a therapist I knew there was a lot she was holding back from me. As a human being I was naturally curious and yet fearful of what my questions would evoke.

So, it was that evening that I set aside time for broaching Moo with some questions. Instead of vanishing out through the cat flap I had recently put in, she stayed sitting on my lap.

"You mentioned something about disturbing my evolution... if you gave me certain information," I began tentatively.

I did... Moo agreed.

"Tell me more."

Moo shifted position and licked her paw, rubbing it over first one eye then the other. I held back from 'therapizing' her movement by saying, 'What is that paw saying?' Or 'what are those whiskers communicating?'

I also held my breath, waiting for Moo to come back to me, until my lungs almost burst.

Moo smiled. Her smile was like physical warmth in the room that gently caressed my skin. *It's alright, I won't run away again...*She sat up and gazed at a point above my head...*It's actually a very long story*, she said. *It would take a lifetime to tell you.*

"I'm listening," I responded.

Well, Moo yawned. Simultaneously, I experienced tautness in her body, which I associated with a high level of alertness. *Human evolution is intimately tied up with animal evolution...*

"Go on…"

She turned and went to nip my finger with her teeth. *Don't rush me!*

"Sorry…"

I take my time because it's hard to translate what I know into your language – which is superficial and has no real depth…You have to remember here that I have to translate the old or rather ancient wisdom into your everyday words…Bits get lost… mainly depth.

"I know. I can understand…"

*I don't think you do understand…*Moo's swift return was almost a growl.

I waited for Moo to continue.

A long time ago – a very long time ago, the Portal or door between the animal world and the human world became locked…This meant that animals could no longer incarnate into human form. This was because the Wise Ones had to withdraw to bring something into being in another – universe or dimension.

"Who were the Wise Ones?" It sounded like something out of a fantasy story.

The Great Cats. She looked at me. *My ancestors, if you like.*

"You mean lions and tigers?"

Yes and no. The big cats you see on the earth are only a pale shadow of the Wise Ones, the 'Elleneron.' All great cats carry the spark, like humans, but have journeyed so far away from their source that it is a pale memory, a dream even.

Moo paused to rub her whiskers with her paw, which I found was a nervous mannerism of hers. *But lately, the last hundred years or so, the door has been forced open. The Elleneron are too far away and involved in this new Project to know about it or close the Portal…"*

"So what's happening, Moo?"

The forcing open of the Portal was created by a desperate need from the animal kingdom to find a way out of their suffering at the hands of various humans. Animal cruelty, you must admit, has reached a terrible level globally…You must know this; it's in your papers, on your news...I know you try to hide papers from me with these documen-taries in, but my whiskers are like antennae that dowse the media. A shudder ran through her. *You see, when the Portal was closed, it was to prevent the carnage that is happening now...It was meant to stop animals coming into human incarnation and, instead, all the animals were to be withdrawn from the planet instead...But now because the Portal is opening, animals that are not ready to incarnate as humans are beginning to come into form – at an alarming rate.*

"Is that such a bad thing?"

Moo growled softly. *Yes, it is a very bad thing...Animals, before they can incarnate as humans, have to become domesticated, that is learn to trust the human race. What is happening now and has been happening for some time, is that animals, incarnating as humans, aren't ready to live amongst the human race. They are too full of fear, which makes them violent, sick and destructive...*

"Are they destructive towards animals?"

*Yes...They're destructive towards all life because they have awareness of who or what they are, they are full of terror. Some of them will leave animals alone. Others are reminded of something when they look at animals and find it too painful so they run away or destroy them...*Moo licked her paw and rubbed it firmly over her ear, *I don't know about you, but I'm starving.*

"Moo!" I implored. "Don't stop now! You've only just begun..."

But I could see daylight had given way to dusk outside. At least an hour had passed since Moo had begun her story. It was at that moment a tin of tuna dropped into my thoughts. And I knew that if I was going to get anything more out of Moo, I had to comply with her wishes...

Chapter Eight

The Purr is an energetic force which underlies all life.
The Gospel of Moo

I knew I needed supervision, which was a requirement of students in training as well as those who were qualified as therapists and practicing. Supervision kept you on track with your clients, as well as highlighting weaknesses that may not have been noticed by the therapist in his relationship with his client. Although any good therapist would have developed an 'internal supervisor' to process his work with his clients, analyzing projections, transferences and counter-transferences sometimes got overlooked. There were times when, for various reasons, one's 'internal supervisor' missed important fragments or would fog over dodgy issues. Supervision, although uncomfortable and irritating at times, was like viewing a therapeutic session through visually enhanced multi-faceted lenses.

The supervision group I belonged to endeavored to meet every four to six weeks. Over the day, interspersed with coffee and lunch, we would discuss any issues of difficulties we were having in our Practice. The work was totally confidential: no names were ever revealed, only the psychological content of a particular session that was troubling the therapist. Prior to the meeting, a supervision paper would have been written and circulated round the group. This served a very good purpose of consolidating material and making what may not seem important, more conscious. It also allowed the group to 'be with' each therapist in their process.

Ali, one of the five members in my group, had actually rung and asked if I was okay. "We haven't seen you for months!" she began in that deep husky voice that I found so attractive, "I wanted to report back to the others that you were still alive...What's been going on for you?"

I trusted Ali. She was a life coach as well as well as therapist. She was also fighting fit with her interest in hockey, basketball and horse riding. We had, until more recently, gone running together regularly and finished off at the pub, sharing news about others we had trained with and talking about that elusive subject of 'settling down' with someone. Although Ali had a nine year old son, she shied away from partnership or getting serious with anyone. She predicted it would only end in disaster as the ancestral lineage she had emerged from, was steeped in disastrous relationships. Her parents, she believed, had hated each other and stayed together just for the sake of the children, while both indulged in a catalogue of short lived affairs outside their marriage. This had instilled in her a desire for freedom at all costs and a distinct lack of trust in relationships. Her brother had, as soon as he could, emigrated to Australia, her sister to America, where she worked as a psychiatrist. She was the only one of the three of them who had settled down with a child. Ali was convinced that the one thing they all had in common was an internal relationship saboteur. Above all, Ali's pockets of freedom amidst her busy life were sacrosanct.

"I've been doing all sorts of things," I responded vaguely. "Time passes so quickly."

"I never see you," Ali persuaded. "Can't we meet sometime? Even if you don't want to come to the supervision, and catch up...You went to Nepal eighteen months ago."

"Two years," I corrected.

"And then I never saw you again...Are you still with that girl you met there?"

"Emmie? No...We finished a long time ago."

There was a pause and then; "Are you well, Pete? I don't mean to pry. But we used to be real buddies and I'm concerned."

"I'm good," I said. "Are you still practicing?"

"Yes, I have four or five clients at the moment – mostly new ones..." Silence stretched between us. Therapists certainly knew how to keep quiet and hold the space! "I am well...I'm sorry about the supervision group, I kept putting it on the back boiler," I explained. "I just wanted a bit of distance from it."

"I can understand that, Pete, everybody has breaks. I'm just wondering if you might be following your old pattern of cutting off from the things you need."

I writhed inwardly and resisted an urge to make some excuse about a client just arriving and that I would ring her back later. The problem was Ali and I knew each other well enough to intuit when excuses were being made. If I told her that I didn't want to talk now, she would accept that and, perhaps, I could ring her back later and explain. But explain what?

Just then the cat flap banged and Moo rushed in with a mouse in her jaws.

"... Is that someone at the door?"

"No," I laughed. "It's Moo – my cat. With a mouse."

"Oh? I can't imagine you with a cat!"

The mouse was shrieking as Moo batted it with her paw.

"Look... I'll ring you back, Ali," I promised. "Are you in this evening?"

"After eight – yes."

"Speak to you again soon."

Moo let the mouse run away and then pounced on it so it shrieked again.

"Oh Moo... take it outside and kill it, for heaven's sake!"

Moo's pupils filled her eyes as she looked up at me. *I'm only playing,* she returned innocently.

"But it's cruel, Moo...It's not as if you're going to eat it...You're just torturing the poor bugger!"

Moo scooped it up in her mouth and I winced as she bit hard down on it and vanished with it through the cat flap. I watched as she stuffed the dead animal in her pouches and thought how she always had to defy and contradict me. Moo had tried to eat a mouse or bird in the past and promptly brought up the half digested remains of fur, feathers and ghoul all over the carpet.

As I had predicted, about ten minutes later, she heaved the contents of her stomach onto the patio, went to drink some water, then slunk under a young willow tree where a few bees were extracting the first rush of pollen from the young catkins. Moo, surprisingly, never went for bees. She would watch them but was never tempted to swat them with her paw. She had once told me that they were a sacred species because of the way they worked and what they produced. They were sacred, Moo had explained, because they had fur and pollinated the planet. More than that, bees had the rare gift of purring. It was their hymn to life. Without bees, she had predicted, civilization would die out because the whole ecosphere would be unhinged. Once I had asked her about their evolution and Moo had responded by saying that they were a species of their own, referring to them as the direct ambassadors of the Gods. She said bees had been there before animal and human races came into being. Often, in the spring and early summer, she would sit under the buddleia in the garden where the bees all congregated and close her eyes. I think at times like this, with her face to the sun, her fur sprinkled with yellow pollen, she was in a truly heavenly place....

Later, when she sheepishly came back into the house, I asked her why she tortured and killed small creatures. On a smaller scale, wasn't it as bad as what we did to animals?

Moo was sitting on the back of an armchair, looking back at me.

It's not as bad – but it still isn't a kind thing to do.

"Why isn't it as bad?"

Well, you're meant to be more evolved than domestic animals, so you have a stronger sense of conscience...

"But you have a conscience, don't you, Moo?"

Moo licked her paw slowly and wiped it over her ear so that it flattened before flipping up again. *Yes, I do... but it is hard sometimes not to give way to these instincts... I am in an animal body.*

"Yes... I have noticed!" I conceded. "And I suppose the temptation must be great at times. Do all animals have a conscience?"

Most of the domestic ones do if they have good experiences with humans and a lot of the wild ones do."

"Which ones have conscience?"

The more evolved ones.

"Like cats, obviously..."

Obviously.

"And?"

Moo sighed, stretched her front and back legs in that painstakingly slow relaxed way that both charmed and infuriated me. *Dogs, and that includes wolves...Horses and elephants. They are all evolved beings...*

I thought. "Hmmm...what about dolphins? They're supposed to have a much bigger brain than the human one."

Moo smiled, like something tickling my soul. *Yes, they do...But you must remember the brain isn't just a physical substance in the body. It's energetic and organic too and so cannot really be measured."* She licked her paw again and sat there with it suspended in mid air as if thinking before putting it down again. *Dolphins belong to another evolutionary stream. They are not only from another time, but from another space..."*

I waited, but Moo didn't venture anything more. "Do you mean they're from another planet?"

You could say that, Moo agreed.

"But if they are from another - umm - evolutionary stream, what are they doing getting caught up in ours? It can't be much fun for them, trapped in fishing nets."

Moo shuddered. *I hope not...Dolphins, like some whales, are here to help. The dolphins,* Moo paused and I felt that spangling zinging sensation of Moo smiling, *they are here to spread joy, disperse some of the depression that hangs over the human race in dark oppressive clouds. Most depression, as you know, is a collective conscience of what has been perpetrated in the name of power and gain, since few people have the capacity to own the conscience collectively, it gets taken on unconsciously by those who are more sensitive.*

I sighed. "Do all animals know this?" I asked.

No – not all animals. Whales are the ancient record keepers. They know the beginning and end of the lineage of evolution...

"It's terrible what we're doing to them then, isn't it?"

Moo flicked her ear. *Yes, it is...*

"What hope is there for us? The human race?"

Moo jumped off the back of the chair and padded across to me, rubbing herself seductively against my chin. Her whiskers tickled my face and seemed to be dowsing my better nature. This time, I waited for the tin of tuna to drop into my mind. "All right, Moo," I said, stroking her. "You'll get what you want. You always do..."

Moo stayed, enjoying the stroking, our intimacy. *There was another reason I caught that mouse today, she said slowly. It wasn't just for play, it was to distract you. I was making it easier for you...*

I thought back to the time Moo had caught the mouse. It already seemed so long ago. Light years away, as if our discussion about evolution had pushed out the boundaries of time as I understood it. Suddenly, I remembered what I had been doing, where I had been standing, talking to Ali about meeting up. I looked back at Moo who held my gaze as if to say *See? Do you understand why I did it now?*

"You were making it easier for me," I repeated.

I gave you the opportunity to withdraw and think... or not think, she added.... *But you must ring Ali back,* she reminded, following me into the kitchen where I had opened the cupboard door and selected a tin of tuna from the two piles there. Since Moo had become a lodger, I bought tuna in bulk when I went shopping. Twelve tins each; hers in brine, mine in oil.

"Oh?" I opened the tin and she jumped up on the surface in

expectation. "Why do I have to ring Ali back?" I forked half the contents of the tin into her bowl. Just recently, I had stopped putting her food down on the floor, because Moo insisted she wanted to eat in a more civilized way. I didn't want to say anything, but I think it was an unconscious move to becoming more human.

Because, Moo responded distractedly...*You have history and a life together...*

"In what way, Moo?"

But Moo didn't answer which was infuriating sometimes because she had aroused my curiosity. But then she rarely answered anything if she was eating tuna. I quickly gave up. I would ask her another time. I checked my watch, four o'clock.

Kirsten would be arriving in another hour, then Tina.

The shrilling of the phone broke into my thoughts. Moo was suddenly beside me in her thoughts as I reached for it: *I know who it is,* she purred throatily.

The moment she said that, I knew who it was too!

"Hi, Pete...Er...I wonder if we could meet up for a coffee sometime," came Kevin's halting voice. "Is that okay?"

I was surprised at how relieved I was to hear his voice. It had been a month since I had heard anything from him. But I drew breath, stopping myself from rushing into something that challenged professional barriers which were in place to keep therapist and client on healthy autonomous ground. But I didn't want to lose Kevin either, now he had returned of his own freewill.

"What about coming round here for coffee?" I suggested.

He hesitated, "I s'pose...I don't know whether I want therapy though."

"I can understand that..."

"I've had a lot of therapy in hospital and I'm worried that it will put me back in those places I don't want to go..." He scraped his throat. "I ... thought we could meet up...As mates..."

"I would like that too." I still had a sense that I was enacting some parental role for him, rather than a merely therapeutic one. "Do you want to stop the therapy then?"

"I thought I had stopped it."

"Well – we left it open. We didn't have a proper closure…"

Kevin hesitated and I worried whether I was pissing him off and whether he could deal with a closure or a real break in therapy.

"Can't we close it over coffee somewhere?"

I hesitated, vacillating because I was about to break with everything I had been taught about the 'therapeutic alliance' and needing to reach closure in the relationship so that the client could claim back their autonomy on a conscious level. It wasn't fair to Kevin more than anything. But 'now' was too fragile to question his autonomy. In the end, decisions were made by the client, not the counselor.

"Yeah…Why not?" I offered.

At that moment, the energy changed between us. The fragility which was there, where neither of us was breathing, had become more bearable. Bugger protocol! Sometimes you had to create you own rules as it went on. I felt a hundred percent authentic in my choice now. "When and where shall we have coffee then, Kevin?"

"I thought tomorrow afternoon."

Damn it! I was full tomorrow afternoon and there was a new client as well.

"I can make it the day after…Wednesday?"

This time there was no hesitation. "Fine! How about Starbucks on Newton Street? At about three!"

"Starbucks at three…" I agreed.

I scribbled on my notepad in red. Not that I was likely to forget.

Slowly, I put down the phone and looked at Moo as she dragged a paw across her whiskers and continued washing herself, saturating her fur with tuna scent as a human adult would splash themselves with aftershave or perfume. She paused, blinking a smile at me as cats do.

"How did you know it was Kevin?"

I have whiskers and they're my dowsing rods. I can pick up what is happening before it becomes visible or audible to you.

I spooned some coffee in to percolate and began cutting several thick slices of bread. Flipping back the tuna lid, I began forking the contents into a pyrex bowl, adding mayonnaise, black pepper and lemon. Cutting slices of cucumber and dicing a spring onion, I piled it all onto one of the hefty slices and clapped on the other slice, pressing it down so tuna squelched out the sides. "Do you know everything, Moo?" I queried, somewhat irritably, as I bit into the sandwich. "I mean is there anything you don't know?"

Of course I don't know everything, Moo responded leisurely, still licking her paw to pass over her ears. *I just know what I need to know...Like you do...*

"But I read papers and watch television, listen to the radio, read books, go to lectures...You just seem to know it..."

Well – it's all out there! Moo said. *If you used your whiskers properly you would know things without going to books and reading newspapers.*

"Are you suggesting I grow whiskers? Would you tell me how to use them, if I did?"

The sort of whiskers that you need to use aren't tangible...They're sort of inner whiskers, an antenna...Like you use when you're being a therapist.

Moo delicately scooped up several pieces of tuna that had dropped off my plate as I was talking. *It isn't so hard...It's just trusting yourself and getting used to working that way. You have to learn to think or dowse the currents of information like animals do...They don't just use their senses, they use their brains which are in the solar plexus. They use an instinctual brain, which they have had to do in order to survive. You just use your human brain, which is full of junk, as I've told you before. It's about not being separate from the rest of life and tuning into a field of interest...It takes practice, like anything. In a way you have to close down your human junk-filled mind and think with your body and senses.* Moo licked up another tuna morsel that had escaped my plate. *It's tuning into the Purr.*

"The Purr? What on earth do you mean, Moo? What Purr?"

The Purr is an energetic force which underlies all life. You probably call it the 'hum'. It is the sound your planet makes, but it's also the sound of the universe. If you lie very still in a quiet place you can hear it...The more you hear it and acknowledge it, the louder it gets until you fall into it.

"And then what?" putting my finished plate on the table, I swung my legs up onto the couch so that I could relax.

Well – you can find out anything you need to know... Moo said, sniffing delicately at the crumbs on my plate and nudging out a tuna morsel to lick up.

"Like what?"

Moo sighed and pushed against my hand, wanting to be stroked. *You listen to things close at hand first... like things that are interacting with your environment... your home. You sort of dowse the energetic field that surrounds you and you know you will get a letter or a phone call within the next half an hour or so, or if you're me, you know that a dog is going to piss on your toilet area just to show they're boss – which they're not. Or you know a mouse is going to zing into those bushes over there, near the dandelion. Your whiskers vibrate and if you're me – you're out there, and if you're me again, you know a new cat is going to move in within the next day or so and is going to come exploring my territory with a view to possession...*

"That's amazing, Moo!"

Moo studied me in that calm appraising way of hers. *It's like anything – you just have to practice and make a space amidst the junk in your head for that Purr to come in. Your greatest problem as a human being is that you're deluded by all the distractions you create for yourself in order to block the Purr out.*

I moved Moo gently so that I could get up and make the coffee, which had percolated nicely, and then I sat down again. "Don't you lose all that ability to dowse the Purr when you become human?"

No – not necessarily. All human life is born with the ability. They just choose not to use it, after a while. A part of your brain shuts down at seven years old for most children. With some it doesn't, and you stay extra sensitive which is painful and you might decide to block it out by doing the drugs thing – just to fit in. Others might go and join a religion whose roots are steeped in the ancient mystery and access the Purr that way. Really the Purr is like one of those things you carry around with you and listen to all day.

"You mean my ipod," I laughed.

Yes…It's not so very different. The Great Purr is like an area of space that becomes filled with things you invite in or you're in touch with.

"So – in your terms it could be called a 'purr-pod'"

Moo licked her paw and I could feel the fine prickling emanation from her of a smile. *Yes, if you like…But I would call it a Moo- pod.*

I smiled back, "A Moo-pod, it is."

I thought of my Buddhist friend, Jenny who was at my supervision group. "I think we might call it something else…The great Om."

Moo's whiskers twitched. *Well you **would** call it something else. Just as you say bees hum instead of purr…It doesn't really matter if it comes from the same source. It works in the same way in that every life form sees God in their own image. You humans see God as a Superhuman, whereas we cats see God as a Supercat. But I know for sure that God has Fur.*

I smiled inside. "I think perhaps you could be right, Moo." I admitted, remembering the warm fuzzy feelings I had experienced throughout my life in my more heightened moments of spirituality.

Moo pluck-plucked at my hand to get me to continue stroking her head. *One of the problems is that you grow a long way from the ground where your natural instincts are....The further you grow from the ground, the taller you become, the harder it is to stay in touch with the Purr. That's why children and animals hear it, because they're close to the ground. .Then old people hear it too, because they're pulled down to the ground by gravity.*

"Moo...Why are you here with me now?"

Moo jumped down suddenly in the way she always did when she wanted to demonstrate the conversation and subject were closed. And I knew at times like this that I was moving too close to fragile ground, just as I did when I was with a client. Again, I was surprised at how strong my feelings around losing Moo were. I also observed, it was a primeval unconscious response rather than a conscious one.

Just before she turned and vanished out of the cat flap she threw back: *You should be contacting that friend of yours now, you have to...You're spending too much time without human company.*

For a while after the cat flap banged, I sat in the silence, mulling over what Moo had said, about the Hum or Purr or whatever it was. Sitting there in the silence, I could almost hear it. But Moo was right – I needed to ring Ali. Even if it was to keep Moo off my back. In a way, I was using my contact with Moo as an excuse not to engage with the world.

Chapter Nine

*Your greatest problem as a human being is that you are deluded by
all the distractions you create for yourself in order to block the Purr
out.*
The Gospel of Moo

I was glad Moo had persuaded me to get back to Ali. I knew my
pattern. When I wasn't sure of doing something, I held back from
committing myself to anything. Time would pass, fuzzing over
the need to take action. And I knew Ali would wait around a bit
for me to call back, but then let it go, taking my absence at face
value, that I wanted to let go of Supervision and her friendship
along with it.

I rang her back, and we agreed to meet up for lunch the next
day, which was Saturday. I had Kirsten and Tina for therapy in
the morning and both my afternoon clients cancelled after Kevin
had phoned.

Tina came to see me just that one more time to tell me how
much better she felt after our initial therapy session. She
admitted something had moved for her during that session, in
the same way the earth's tectonic plates move and reform the
landscape. I was pleased for her if it had, but was not entirely
convinced that this could happen to a 'sophisticated' client like
Tina. It was more likely that she felt a little out of her depth with
me and had decided to cool it for a while. In reality, I don't know
how many clients I've had who have only made the first session.
I'm not judgmental about this. The psychotherapeutic alliance is
a tangible, visceral thing where the 'whole' of you is held and
seen.

I have to admit it was with a mixture of relief and disappointment that Kirsten rang me and said she didn't need to see
me any more, because she was now in regular dialogue with

Moo, through the *Mooisphere*, no doubt. And within this context, I experienced guilt because I was a complete coward when it came to discussing other people's experiences of Moo. I was a real Pontius Pilate in my betrayal of the real and beautiful. Oscar Wilde's words came back to haunt me again and again, 'Each man betrays the thing he loves.'

With some clients you get a gut feeling, right from the beginning whether they're going to stick around or leave early on. It's an energetic thing and I know Moo would agree with me on this, but the bottom line was, I needed to have clients to pay my bills and, it seemed Moo was sabotaging this by her presence. I'd have to speak to her about her ongoing tuna supply. I bet if that were threatened, she would keep her paws off my clients!

But, one thing I knew was that I would see Kirsten again, some time in the future.

Ali lived on a small dairy farm. One that had been in her family generations and which, despite ongoing structural problems in the cottage and the shifting of the oak beams, she was reluctant to leave. Just seven cows remained, a clutch of free-range chickens, four goats and her two horses. She was in the stable, talking to her stable hand, Joey, a fourteen-year-old with short spiky hair and a gold earring in his right ear. Even before she turned round and that mane of auburn hair framed her face, I could smell her scent, a mixture of horse, patchouli and spice. A body smell that was unique to her and which I remembered from the time when we were in training.

She swung round as Joey's gaze slid across her shoulder to me and she was just the same Ali. A few grey hairs streaked her hair but she was earthy and comfortable in her body as I remembered.

She gave me one of those rib crushing hugs she was well known for, then reached up to brush her lips against my cheek. She drew back, looking at me. "Oh – *You* haven't changed," she remarked. "Still the tall, dark handsome guy that I remember from that induction day!"

I grinned and slapped her on the back. "You always did damage to my ego!" I said. "You look pretty good yourself, Ali."

She took my hand and led me towards the old slate cottage that was bigger on the inside than it looked. "Come on...I've just brewed some coffee and my boy's just made a wealth of flapjacks."

"So he's well trained," I said, liking the way I immediately felt at home with her. There was none of the often arduous searching for something neutral to say or endless questions that delayed intimacy.

"Patrick's more than well trained," she bragged. "He adores cooking. He certainly didn't get that from me...And he's good at it too. Brill, in fact," she grinned. "Although I might be a bit biased...Would you believe, he's coming up to ten now?"

I shook my head. "He'll soon be a young man."

Inside the kitchen, heated by an ancient Aga that had perhaps been there before the cottage was built, it was warm and cozy and I suddenly felt famished as the sweet smell of freshly baked bread and homemade soup curled its way down into my stomach. "God – that smells good!" I exclaimed.

She poured the coffee into an Earthenware mug and pushed it towards me along with a plate of flapjacks, still warm from baking. "Hungry?"

"I am now..."

She smiled as a boy appeared in the doorway with the same deep auburn hair and clear blue eyes. A slash of freckles covered his nose and cheeks. "Hi," he invited.

"Hi," I returned, my mouth full. "These flapjacks are amazing!"

He grinned. "You are staying for lunch, aren't you?"

"You bet I am," I enthused." If lunch is as good as this...It could be hard to get rid of me."

"Don't forget to wash your hands," Ali reminded Patrick as he reached to slice the bread.

I hadn't realized how much I had missed scenes of domesticity and the warmth this could evoke until then. The kitchen was even homelier than I had remembered with squat bunches of shallots, onions and dried herbs hanging neatly from the blackened wooden beams. Shiny copper pans, plates and cutlery clung to the faded paintwork on either side of the Aga. There was an old wind-up Grandfather clock ticking royally between two mullioned windows. An assortment of old chipped and colorful bottles caught the light on a shelf. These were the treasures Ali would collect on the old farmland when she was rotavating an area to grow onions and root vegetables. I knew the kitchen was where everything happened for Ali; where she wrote her letters, essays and supervision papers, shelled home grown peas and broad beans. It was a window into a life that our modern world had left far behind. And one we all craved to return to all the same. How easy it was to override the sustaining influence of simple things like a woodstove, homemade products and companionship for the latest gadget or fix in our modern diseased age.

Joey came in later to have his soup and bread. Although he'd washed his hands, the nails were ingrained with dirt. I recognized the sharp pungent smell of goat's milk on his clothes along with horse manure.

"Joey wants to work with animals, when he's older." Ali explained. "At least he's had a lot of experience here."

Joey nodded shyly and said, his mouth still full, "I want to work with big animals rather than small ones," he finished.

I met Ali's eyes across the table and she was smiling back at me. "The young are so sure of what they want and where they want to go in life...Do you ever remember being like that?"

"None of my youthful desires to be rich and famous came to much," I admitted. "Because I thought too big." I looked at Joey. "Your dreams can be realized and you're already working towards their realizations...I can only wish you the best."

"I want to be a Chef," Patrick announced determinedly, smearing a hunk of bread round his bowl to extract the last of the soup from his bowl. And I want to have my own restaurant one day."

"Now why doesn't that surprise me?" Ali laughed, ruffling his hair fondly. "I think it's a wonderful thing to do."

"People are always going to want food," Joey agreed. "You're never going to be out of business."

"Well I for one," I admitted, "am going to eat at your restaurant."

Patrick grinned and held out his hand. "A deal?" he said.

"A deal," I echoed.

"So, is there a man around?" I asked later, as we followed a footpath that led us by a small canal.

"No.....Actually – I was going to add, 'not likely' because they never seem to last five minutes with me."

"I can't believe that," I said, falling into step with her.

Ali inclined her head affirmatively. "It's true...I remember reading in a book, *Clan of the Cave Bear*, that the heroine, Ayla, had a totem, which was too strong for any man...I think that's why they never stay around me for long...My totem's too strong!"

"What is your totem?"

I don't know...But I have a feeling it could be a big bear," she said, simulating the shuffling lunging gait of the animal.

I plucked a blade of long grass and chewed on the end of it, the bittersweet taste reminded me of my childhood. "Do you want one to stay?" I asked, "or are you using the totem thing as an excuse?"

"I don't think I've found the right one yet. Or..."

"Or?" There was a break in the clouds and the sudden burst of sunshine on the stream was almost blinding. "Or what?" But I knew what she was going to say before she spoke.

"Maybe.... I'm chasing after the wrong sex!"

"You still feel like that?" I tried, remembering that she had sometimes shared this at intervals throughout her training, that she found women attractive and wasn't sure which way she swung. This had invited other students to voice the same uncertainty about their sexuality, including male ones. At the end of it, we had concluded that in all honesty most of us were attracted to the same gender at some time in our lives, but this didn't mean that it had to be acted out.

"There was someone – a woman about eighteen months ago," she began breathlessly. We had stopped by the water as if mesmerized by its coruscating surface. "Her name was Linda and she was five years older than me. She was surer about what she was doing and what she wanted than I was. I wasn't her first female relationship although she was married to a man that she was happy with." Her voice had dropped and I heard wistfulness, sadness in the timbre. "She wanted something more serious. But I felt out of my depth, out of control…And there was Patrick."

"What was it like for you?"

There was a brief silence and then Ali turned round to face me, blue eyes vulnerable and yet full of emotion too. "It was…Amazing, wonderful, scary," she sighed. "But I felt as if I was traveling at a speed the rest of me couldn't keep up with."

"You broke it off," I finished.

She nodded and, involuntarily, tears bounced onto her cheeks, glittering like small prismatic jewels in the afternoon sun. "It was painful…So very painful."

"I'm sorry…"

"It was beautiful," she went on, not hearing me. "I have never felt so alive." She turned back to me. "I think I'm still longing for that…Missing it."

"Is there any chance?"

"No – not really." She grimaced. "It was a typical fairytale romance. I went to stay with my sister, Sally, in Houston…Linda and her husband were invited over for dinner one evening, it was a romantic evening with us all sitting outside in the garden watching the sun go down, the breeze in the trees. We'd all had a bit too much to drink and spoke freely, without inhibitions. Linda made the first move. She held my hand under the table." She swallowed." We clicked straightaway and I suppose Linda did all the running...I felt like a teenager again. We just had a wonderful two week romance and then I came back," she grimaced again. "End of story."

In the distance a curlew sounded a haunting cry through the trees and somewhere behind us another answered.

I took her elbow, "Except it wasn't the end."

"It was..." she swallowed. "But it opened something up inside me – a longing a hunger for deeper connection." She shook her head. "I don't regret it or anything, I'm glad I had that relationship, but I couldn't have carried on in that way. It..." her chin trembled, "I don't want you to feel sorry for me here...It just leaves me with myself, which is feeling lonely." The sun went behind a cloud and we felt the chill in the air. It was still only February. And there was frost on the grass on the other side of the bank where the sun hadn't reached.

"Perhaps I better be going," I said.

"Why?" Ali called me back.

I shrugged. "You'll want to spend time with Patrick. We've both got clients tomorrow." And then there was Moo.

"How about another time?" she suggested. "We could go riding together?"

"Yeah, okay...That would be good. When?"

She bit her lip as we slowly made our way back to the cottage. "How about after Supervision, next Friday, it's the weekend then."

I caught my breath, "You're rather assuming that I'll go to Supervision..."

She looked at me. "I think you need it, Pete. We both do."

The distant whinnying of the gelding, followed by the louder more insistent one of Monty, the Shire horse called us back from each other. "They need my attention," she said. "And I think Monty wouldn't mind another ride. He loves going through the woods at this time of the day, picking up all the scents of animals that have passed that way. Deer, fox, sometimes badger..." The whinny came again and she whistled back in response. "I'll see you next Friday at Supervision," she invited with finality.

"It looks like it."

"Don't forget your paper." She suddenly squeezed my arm. "I've really enjoyed spending time with you. Like old times."

"The feeling's mutual."

The horses whinnied, this time, in unison, and Ali was quickening her pace as she walked towards the field where they were. I started after her, torn, and then before I could stop myself: "Do you understand your horses when they speak to you like that?"

She stopped briefly and frowned. "Of course I do. Why shouldn't I?"

"I just wondered if you could really understand what they're communicating in words?"

She looked at me and I stared back wishing I'd kept my mouth shut. But that was the whole thing about therapy or relationships of any kind for that matter. Things that you'd held back and wanted to say slipped out last minute, always at the end of the session. Within the ending there was no real ground, or it was mutually accessible. It was safe then to ask questions, to say things that had seemed too much or stupid at the time.

"No, not exactly," her voice trailed off as her mobile burst out with a set of whinnying calls.

"Doesn't matter," I said quickly, reaching in my pocket for the car keys. "See you next week."

She waved, already engrossed in the call. The horses went on whinnying..

Chapter Ten

Each life form sees God in their own image. You humans see God as a Super Human… whereas we cats see God as a Super Cat. But I know for sure that God has Fur.
Gospel of Moo

Unease filled me when I let myself back into the house. Would Moo forgive me for leaving her so long? I had been gone hours. The unease increased when a thorough search of the house revealed all Moo's usual basking spots, hidey-holes and window ledges empty. Was Moo angry? Had she run away and left me? It had dawned on me several times that I wasn't an individual in this equation. Being with Moo was like being married without the sex. And how many sexless marriages did therapists hear about in the privacy of the therapy room?

Moo slept on my bed and, sometimes, if it was very cold, both of us burrowed into the feather down of the duvet for warmth. She also slept on top of me, often impervious of where she sank her claws in the midst of one of her long ecstatic purring episodes. She licked me awake, starting at my eyes and then my mouth, if I didn't move immediately. If she was unhappy with something, she would leap off my bed, sharpen her claws on the carpet before she left or, even worse, leave me one of those Moo farts which seemed to cling to every natural or manmade fiber in the room. We ate together and were frequently in dialogue.

So even though Moo had encouraged me to seek Ali out, I still wasn't sure how Moo would react when I got back this late.

There was a dead mouse on the kitchen floor and as I suspected, one in my trainer, which I emptied out. Moo very rarely caught one mouse at a time. She would discover a nest and gradually bring them in over two or three days. Often, she would hide them in places that were difficult to find or the injured mouse had escaped to find sanctuary under the cooker. Over the subsequent days a faint musty smell would give way to a gassy more pungent odor that wouldn't go away, I would hunt out the poor dead creature which was usually trapped under the sofa, under the cooker, washing machine or fridge.

One of the worst and most memorable events was when I had gone with a mate to watch Manchester playing Liverpool in a football match and we had stayed out late drinking and celebrating. Both of us were lost in the euphoria of the Manchester supporting crowds. We had staggered back to my flat and collapsed almost unconscious, Mickey on the sofa, and me in the hallway at the bottom of the stairs, not trusting myself to go upstairs to my bed.

Moo had pluck-plucked me into waking consciousness where my head felt it was going to explode with the pressure of the hangover mixing with my medication. I felt as if I was in a goldfish bowl watching the world swim in and out of view. In the next room, I found Mickey in a semi-stupefied state staggering around in his underpants with one foot in his jeans, hanging up on an enraged girlfriend, convinced that he had been with another woman. I could vouch for him, but I didn't fancy his chances. Just as he was making his way through the kitchen into the hall, I saw something hanging from the bottom of his shoe: something squashed, bloody and red with ears and a tail.

On discovering it, Mickey had unwittingly pulled off the remains then dived into the toilet to throw up in the pan. Several times since we had gone to football together, but he had never stayed over again and neither of us mentioned the incident again.

I noticed Moo hadn't touched her Munchies as I went to open the back door. There was no answering call as I looked out on the small garden. Dry leaves scurried across the patio as a thin breeze keened through the willow branches. It was bright outside, incandescent. I looked up at the moon, round and full, and relaxed a little. Full moon! Moo had said long ago that all cats stay out at full moon. *It's a natural thing,* Moo had told me. *The whole of nature responds to this. It's a reorientation to what's important. Some humans even use the moon cycles. But it's also a potentially dangerous time…*

Closing and locking the door, I was able to release my deep concerns of Moo abandoning me and I climbed the stairs slowly, overcome by sudden weariness.

It seemed only five minutes later after falling asleep that I awoke, my heart pounding with a mixture of anxiety and fear. There was so much light in the room that I thought it was daylight and, then looking at the clock, saw that it was three o'clock exactly, I realized it was early morning. I hadn't got round to drawing the curtains and the swollen face of the moon was a searchlight sweeping my room. Leaning across, I drew the curtains, but the light glowed incandescently through the material.

Moo? Where was Moo?

Just at that moment, she sprang noiselessly up onto my pillow, startling me. I reached out and asked, "Where have you been, Moo? You've been gone ages!"

Moo's fur was cold, crisp and smelled of night air and moonlight.

She rubbed against my hand and then settled herself on my chest, purring down at me, her eyes huge and round like the moon. *I've been busy,* she said.

"Doing what? Besides moon bathing?"

Moo batted my nose playfully. *Working, of course!*

I knew better than to undermine what she was saying by pulling some joke about her working abilities. Underneath that playful 'bat' were sharp retracted claws that could do damage. And I wasn't in a very good position to defend myself if Moo lost her temper. Moo in the throes of one of her irritable or angry moods was something to behold. She veered towards the wild and animalistic rather than the civilized.

She licked her paw, waiting for me to coax more information out of her.

"Go on then," I invited. "I'll tell you what I've been doing, if you tell me what you've been doing."

I know what you've been doing! Moo responded in a flash. She poured an earlier image of me with Ali into my mind. I watched it become animated and take shape before me. I could see the interior of the cottage kitchen; myself bending over a soup bowl and smiling; Ali looking across at me and the two boys kicking each other under the table. Later I could hear myself asking Ali if she really understood what her horses were asking.

I looked at Moo and rubbed my eyes. "Was that your memory, or mine? It's so real."

Because it is real, Moo countered. *It's not yours or my memory, it's ours...*

"Does that mean..."

Yes, it does, Moo licked her paw nonchalantly. *Everything you experience I have access to.*

"That's not fair, Moo... It's an invasion of privacy."

Moo continued licking her paw and looked down at me. *It works two ways, you know.*

"How?"

But I already knew.

I can't force my experience onto you, Moo began.

"Because that would be interfering with my evolution," I finished for her.

But, I can invite you to share it.

I sighed. "Go on then."

Moo stopped licking her paw and placed it carefully back on the duvet. *Are you sure?* She seemed both excited and hesitant. *Do you want to see my work tonight? What I've been doing?*

I sighed. "Yes, as long as it doesn't involve catching poor defenseless mice."

Moo made a deep sound at the back of her throat which came

out somewhere between a growl and purr. *Close your eyes then...*

At first there was nothing, just the sound of wind rattling the bare branches of the trees outside, the grate of a can rolling along the street outside. I was aware of Moo's breath against my eyes, warm and familiar.

And then suddenly...

There was an explosion that seemed to suck all the air out of the room, out of my lungs. Involuntarily, my body began to vibrate violently, starting at my head, then down my neck and torso to my pelvis and legs. I drew breath as the vibrating slowly died away. Something opened at the back of my neck like a trap door. And then colors and sounds rushed into the opening so that I felt I was choking, suffocating.

While this was going on, another part of me was ranting on about this being ridiculous. This wasn't happening in normal reality. It was like tripping, something I hadn't experienced for years. Then I remembered an out-of-body experience I had when I was very ill with pneumonia as a boy. Up until this moment, I had shelved the unfolding images away somewhere at the back of mind. I'd been looking down at this fourteen year-old-boy on the bed, his skin filmed in sweat and I had seen a woman sitting by his head, holding his hand and talking to him. It had taken me a few weeks to discover that that figure sitting patiently by my bed was my mother. And then something in me had culled the memory.

I was aware again of the room, of Moo perched on my chest, purring gently. *You're safe,* she tried to assure me. *Go back into that place when you were a boy lying on the bed ill and I'll show you what happened.*

Reluctantly, I fell back into that space.

Time unreeled as a cine film. It stopped and I saw myself idling along the street in school uniform towards home. I had wandered off my usual territory into an area of squat terraced houses pushed so closely together that they looked as if they were holding their breath. Yet, perhaps it was me, that boy, holding his breath. My heart was thudding, yet I felt as though I had become part of a cine film playing in the dark of a cinema. I had a presentiment of what was going to happen. I was aware of being both schoolboy and observer, of the fizz and prickle of hair on my neck. I was being followed. I could see that in the way the shadows jerked forward and back as they tracked me. Three shadows, boys. Watching, I felt my heart sounding out a troubled tattoo as I mentally urged the boy that was me to hurry. Run! For God's sake run! The feet shadowing the boy were noiseless, invisible. But several times the boy who was me, turned and glanced round uneasily before quickening his pace.

And then the three older boys, wearing navy blue balaclavas, had surrounded the boy, closing in on him as they knocked the satchel from his shoulder, made him empty out his pockets on the oil stained pavement and kicked him down to the ground. Quickly, they made off with his satchel, his keys, money, every-thing he had, shouting after him that if he should breathe a word about this, they would kill him. This was merely a warning.

Perspiration filmed my brow as I watched the film script unroll. The boy picked himself up, dusted himself down, dabbed at the blood that was leaking through the tear in his trousers and limped back in the direction that he knew would lead him home.

His mother had chided him for coming home in such a state, although even then her relief that he was all right overrode the telling-off she could have given him. What on earth had made him follow that way through town, into an area that was rough and violent and in a time when mobile phones were just a fantasy?

Time passed. He followed the boy's progress, which was him with a mixture of fascination and concern. His wounds, although superficial in the form of bruises, abrasions and cuts, had wounded him more deeply. His youthful trust in life had been ruptured and hung by a fine thread to the structure of everyday.

He had retreated into himself. And there were internal fears writhing like phantoms inside him. Phantoms that clutched at his heart. It was as if there was a hole inside him into which all the bad stuff of the world, the emotional carnage, used as a dumping ground. His dreams were dark, menacing and somehow haunting. As soon as he felt he had forgotten them, they would rise up from nowhere and assault him.

One night he had a dream, although he seemed to be fully awake at the time. The dream took place in his bedroom. He'd just thrown all his books down on the floor after school and collapsed on the bed when he was aware of two surreal figures standing at the foot of his bed. He sensed their intent, drew back from their conflicting ice and fire.

One resembled an old picture book image of Jack Frost. The skin was cool ice green, the fingernails sharp and chiselled. Its hair was set in short sharp ice crystals that clinked together whenever it moved. And the eyes were dark caverns containing the tiniest pinprick of fluorescent light. The other form glowed in crimson. Sulphur and orange. As the other was cold as ice, this one burned, scorched when it drew close to the boy who withdrew for his own safety. They were arguing, their voices deep and high, sharp and blunt. They were arguing over him in hideous strident howls and ear shattering roars. He wanted to close his eyes, but the two figures seemed imprinted on his retina, even though his eyes were closed. He knew his body was both fiery and frozen.

The air hissed as the fiery one raised his hand to strike the cool green manikin of the ice and the atmosphere seemed to sizzle, crackle and burn. Shivering with fear and conflicting body temperature, the boy clamped his hands over his ears in an effort to block out the sound, but the sound moved through him.

And when he looked again, the figures had gone. There was just the smell of acrid smoke and thick swampy water that festered and bubbled. He groaned with pain and frustration because he knew that the two compelling figures were inside him. His body was their battleground. And they were fighting for their own lives rather than his.

My life...My life! The boy had held onto this reality through gritted teeth. *Not their life.* And yet he knew that if he tried to fight them with anger and fear, they would grow stronger through it. They would suck his anger and fear from him and use it to overcome his will and drain his spirit. This he knew within the deepest recesses of his being, in the place where he was pure spirit, rather than camouflaged by boyhood and his humanness. At some point as the fire and ice tore through him, pulling him apart fiber by fiber, organ by organ, he let go...

He was in his bed but floating above it at the same time and there was a white bird at the window. It could have been a dove, or eagle, or even a seagull. All he cared about was that it was white and pure and it could take him away from this battle-ground where his spirit and physical form were lodged. He was in his soul body and that's what they were fighting for...His soul.

The bird stretched its wings as it carried the boy through the window and out and out into the still dew of the night air – where there was no fighting. Only the quiet beauty of the ancient stars.

The bird took him far away to places he had never seen that were too beautiful for words and to foreign lands where people spoke different languages and had different colored skin.

"I am a soul bird," the bird had spoken. "I will protect you and when you wake up, you will be well again."

"I don't want to wake up," the boy, who was himself, mumbled. "I want to stay with you."

The bird shuddered beneath him, making him grip the feathers harder. "They all say that," the bird said. "But I am not here to take you away...I am here to return you safely to your own life, the body that has been bequeathed to you for your work. You have important work to do, boy."

The boy was becoming sleepy with all that he had seen and experienced. And the last question he asked before he found himself in his own room and bed was; "Who are you? And how will I find you again?"

"I will find you," the bird's distant cry reached him, as the boy fell into the deep and dark silence of the room again and slept.

Much later, I opened my eyes and found Moo was lying beside me on the pillow. One eye opened as she saw that I was awake. The moon was still filling the room with its ghostly incandescence and the clock read three thirty-one. I picked it up, then shook it in disbelief. I felt as if I had been away hours, days, and weeks. Sitting up and switching the light on I winced, acknowledging the sharp pounding in my temples. I felt beaten up; every muscle fiber in my body stretched to breaking point as if I'd spent the last few hours hauled across a torture rack.

As images from the dream, came rolling in relentlessly in a tide of impressions, I felt myself reach out to them questioningly yet, recoil from them too. Within me, I experienced all the confusion and disorientation of someone who had time traveled or emerged from hibernation. This was worse than any jet lag I had known.

I know you feel awful. Moo began. *And I'm sorry.*

I said nothing, just clasped my forehead in my hands. I had never heard Moo apologize for some action that she had performed. I rested in the space between us.

I think you probably had too much there.

"You bet I did," I agreed.

I just wanted to show you the sort of work I do. That's what I was doing last night and especially at the full moon. That's when the energy of the earth becomes open to outside influences that can swing either way. It's just raw unharnessed energy that needs to be tamed, which can be used for good as well as for bad.

I shook my head, wondering if I was still dreaming. "Moo! That is amazing work. You keep people safe! You protect them!"

Moo made that funny sound at the back of her throat that I had come to understand indicated that she was pleased with my progress, as a teacher would when working with a mentally challenged pupil.

Cats are particularly good at this work. More so than other animals because they are more likely to be domesticated. Wolves are good at it too and horses. Wolves will howl which keeps the spirits away. You see it's not a matter of you owning us, feeding and protecting us. In many ways, it's the other way around.

"I see that now, in fact you've always done that."

I thought about the great witch burnings in the Middle Ages, where thousands of cats were burned or drowned with their owners. True witches, as a friend of mine who had done a PhD in the origin of Wicca had once told me, were healers. They used their powers to help those in the community who were suffering mentally, physically and emotionally. Their healing powers were protective and enlightening. They would exorcise the demons of the mind and body. The demons were still very real and tangible today in more tribal communities of the world in parts of Africa, Indonesia and the Amazon. Cats basically protected those in their community that were linked to them. They were, in actuality, psychic therapists.

I knew from my research into the roots of counseling and psychotherapy that they had emerged from a much older tradition of healing and medicine. This tradition was embedded deep within the matrix of world culture and underpinned the diversity of so called 'primitive' healing techniques, such as shamanism. Basically, the shaman was the tribal logos around which the group constellated. The shaman was well known and respected throughout the world from Siberia, to the Inuit communities, the Sami people, the Aborigines to Africa and the North American Indians. Unlike psychology and counseling today, which was fast becoming a popular career choice, very few people wanted to become a shaman. It was a mantle that involved extreme suffering on all levels of being. And yet it was this source of suffering which became the criteria for passage into this realm that involved communication between the spirit world and the realm of the Gods.

But usually the shaman was 'called' to take on the role in many different ways throughout their life. This calling often presented itself through bodily dis-ease which became increasingly and progressively more debilitating until the call was answered and received. In the modern day world this could be through bipolar disorder, depression, even schizophrenia.

Shamanism could present itself through ancestral lineage or through some disfigurement or incapacity, which would make it hard for the person to engage in a normal everyday life. On a psychic level they could be subject to hearing voices or become 'possessed' which would not abate until the shaman 'initiate' responded to the call of his destiny.

The shaman would gain insight into a patient's condition by descending or ascending the 'world tree' and entering upper and lower realms of experiential contact with spirits, gods or demons. Within his shamanic trance he would sometimes voluntarily take on the patient's illness to gain understanding of it and learn from the spirits what needed to be done in order to alleviate the disease. Sickness in the body and mind were inseparable. It was the shaman's task to align the patient with meaning, purpose and values by appeasing the spirits or Gods that were looking after his patient's destiny. This alignment became the opening for the patient's future life work.

The shaman was both religious and practical, and within societies shaped around such healers there was no division between religion and science. The shaman's ability to take on their patient's condition still happens in the modern world through humanistic, transpersonal and psychospiritual therapies. This is true alchemy where the therapist takes on the condition of the client in order to understand it better. He 'holds' the condition, allowing the client to step outside the imprisoning restraints of his personality and view it with detachment. The therapist literally becomes the change agent. Homeostasis between the client's intrapsychic and interpersonal world occurs as a result of the interaction between therapist and client.

With the introduction of the Descartian-Newtonian mechanistic model which shaped the world view in the 17th century, the Gods and spirits were exiled as the scientific model left its imprint on the emerging mechanistic template. Yet, as Carl Jung asserted; at the point that the Gods and Spirits were exiled from the Western world, they became internalized in the psyche of the patient instead. These so-called 'aberrations' became enlisted under the rapidly emerging labels of neuroses and hysteria."

With the advent of a more mechanistic era, the shaman healer became exiled to the wings, while the scientist in the form of the priest doctor became foreground and centre stage.

Moo was purring as she was reading my thoughts: *Basically you're very sick as a race, because you have exiled or killed off your guardians – those who would keep you safe. So you get a lot of people like Kevin who are open to all these psychic influences, yet have no tools to use them or protect themselves from them...*Moo seemed to sigh. *That's why many of the lost young people gravitate to animals like us – because they sense we understand them and can offer them healing.*

As the dark globe of the night turned, the moonlight incandescence never wavered. The last question I remembered asking Moo before I finally gave into my exhaustion was about the white bird. "Who was that white bird?"

The white bird was your guardian – your protector when you were a child.

"And you are my protector now," I said to myself as I sank back into the welcome peace of oblivion.

Chapter Eleven

You see it's not a matter of you owning us, feeding and protecting us. In many ways, it's the other way around.
Gospel of Moo

It is strange how easily transpersonal experiences slip into the background, especially as they are so richly imbued with color and meaning at the time. It is not as if they are easily forgotten, it is as if they belong to another time and place that you can't always find your way back to. It reminds me of someone who has died and you've felt close to. At first, the whole cine film of their life unfolds before you as your memory becomes saturated with their presence, the features and conditions of their lives. For a while you seem to become them as you live their mannerisms, their longings, fears and hopes. Then, after saturation, you let go and their memory is released into that place which is rarely accessible again.

Moo never referred to that experience in the future. It was as if it had never happened outside the context of a dream...

Thankfully, I allowed myself to be sucked up into the kaleidoscope of life again so that there was no empty space or, as Moo called it, I was filling my mind with junk in order to avoid union with the Purr, or the union that I craved.

I received the supervision papers from the group and sent mine off after much re-writing and deliberation.

There were five of us altogether. Delilah-the-Rottweiler who, as always, managed to shame us all with her abundance of clients. In her paper, she said she saw eighteen each week and, reluctantly, had to turn down three because she had been laid low with a chest infection. A devout lesbian and proud of it, most of her clients were either following suit or unsure about their own sexuality. I would imagine that the few who had any apprehensions about their sexuality, came to a speedy decision either way after spending time with Delilah, who would unearth anything unconscious and spread it out on the therapeutic slab for all to see. As a woman, she was attractive with her curvaceous figure and cantaloupe melon breasts. Her voice was husky from all the cigarettes she smoked and sexy in a strange sort of way. Her mouth was wide and full-lipped, her nose small and freckled and her eyes a deep and moody sea green. Her naturally blonde hair was streaked with shades of gold and red and spiked out. There was a silver stud in her left nostril and one on her belly button, which always showed when she stretched. She wore blue cords and matching T-shirt and desert boots. Her nickname came from her way of getting hold of something you had said or not said and not letting go until she was satisfied with the answer. Satisfaction, she had openly admitted, wasn't easy too come by! Her weakness came from not being able to accept that she was ever wrong. This she openly admitted to, yet found criticism so difficult that she had to always be on the defense. Her history revealed an abusive father who had physically whipped her with his belt every time she annoyed him, and a mother who was too doped up on tranquillizers to notice what was happening between her only daughter and husband. Delilah had run away from home twice without much success, and suffered the humiliation of being brought back to the refuge, that wasn't a refuge each time, kicking and screaming. Finally at eighteen, she had dyed her hair and run off to London. There, despite all the drug temptations, she had held her own, worked her way from being a toilet attendant at British Rail to a waitress and finally a train driver at twenty. On a good salary and willing to work long hours she bought a flat with a girlfriend and lived in Camden Town for several more years. Finally, she had returned to her hometown after finding out her mother had drunk herself to death and her father had been imprisoned for manslaughter. She inherited the house with all its memories, quickly sold it and bought a flat somewhere in Didsbury, where she had lived for the past ten years.

'Green Jilly', as we called her, had her seven regulars beside co-editing Green Forever Green Books, a small and active publishing company, embracing ecopsychology and supporting various tree projects. Besides that, she was co-running wilderness workshops for teenagers living in deprived areas on the outskirts of inner cities.

Jilly was small in build with mouse colored longish hair, braided at the front, and wearing Swedish clogs and cotton purple baggy trousers in typical 60s style. Aside from being vegan, she also spent time at the local Buddhist group and even found time to cook food for the weekend get-togethers. Her brown eyes were troubled and soft, restless and sentimental. She grinned at me when she saw me and gave me a hug. "Great to see you again, Pete," she enthused. "Sorry I haven't been in touch."

I hugged her back.

Gino, in his early thirties, was a gorgeous hunk of an Italian with that olive skin, dark hair, brown eyes and a well-oiled body that was used to working out. A body that any woman, or man for that matter, would die for. I was shocked when I learned that he was a vicar, admitting that I had a mindset about vicars being bald headed, spectacled and weedy looking characters with goofy yellowing teeth. But Gino had taken time out from the clergy when he did his training, a time out that was still in place, five years later. He had twelve regular clients, young lads that were in some sort of spiritual and existential crisis. I always felt comfortable with Gino because his presence was calming and therapeutic.

Introducing myself back into the fold, I felt like a black sheep. But thankfully, Delilah, if she had any thoughts about the clients I presented, held back from her usual barrage of questions and challenges. She just asked me where Kevin was now. Did I still see him?

"No, not often…It's always on his terms anyway."

"How does it feel to meet a client, as an acquaintance?"

I returned her gaze. "Unique," I said smiling.

Delilah hung on tentatively. "Why are you meeting? For yourself or for Kevin?"

"Both," I responded honestly.

After the session, we all went to an Italian restaurant as we always did and over a few glasses of wine relaxed into pleasant banter and gossip about others in the training. We talked about past students who had graduated after us, those that had quit the training or quit being therapists and what they were doing instead. Then we talked about our tutors and what they were doing. Most of them we remembered with fondness because, like us, they were struggling with domestic, financial and emotional difficulties equal to our own. Of course, during the first two years of our training our tutors were sacrosanct, perfect, beyond condemnation and fault as were all role models. Slowly, insidiously, cracks began to make their presence known in that perfect veneer and as our role models became tarnished with commonplace weaknesses, flawed with the same longings, relationship problems and yearnings as our own, they fell from Grace. Embittered, we had judged and condemned them for their ordinariness, angry that we could have believed them to be anything other than normal. Our role models had accepted our punishing wall of shame and fallen ideation flatly, without fighting back until we realized that it was part of 'the journey'. One we had all been on for too long. Somehow it made it worse that we could see how we had projected our longings and unfulfilled needs on our tutors in the hope of having them reciprocated. Needs that had been unfulfilled in our own childhood and journey into adolescence. But somehow, psychological awareness had prized open the black box where everything could remain hidden, before rendering all that had been asleep and unconscious awake and conscious. Being conscious, as we had found was painful, excruciatingly so. Where there had been someone or something to blame before, there was no blame only the healing that could come through owning our own imperfections and mess. The worst thing about being conscious, was that it was almost impossible to become unconscious again. No wonder our trainers bore our scars. And yet, owning our own mess was an oblique way of taking control, hauling back the tide of our projections and, instead, becoming grounded in them. The strength that came from this process, of owning our faults and weaknesses, released a newfound strength. And that was the whole point behind the therapeutic process, not to cut off from the past as was so endemic in the West, but to bring that which had been shameful and unbearable into the present. Use it as a tool to shape a new path. Your own path. Not your parents', nor your peers'. Ancestral fault lines were no longer something that carried shame and blame. They were scars that scored the soul, making you stand out as a warrior and teacher instead of someone weak and oppressed. In psychological terms, we had introjected self-worth from the mirroring our tutors had held up to us throughout the training. Nothing had changed, except our belief in ourselves. This was a process that we would duplicate in our relationship with our clients. Our clients had to fall in love with us, make us their role models, accepting our mirroring as we accepted their projections and transferences. But as they became ultimately strengthened by our commitment to each other, we became weakened by their emerging strength. This was the nature of therapy, the ultimate alchemy of the psyche or the soul, reminding me of the person who had touched Christ's garment to receive healing and Christ weakened, had known. Not that we held delusions of grandeur in being Christ or Buddha-like, but our clients had to idolize us, fall in love with us for a while, in order to see themselves as they really are. And now, after all this projection, anger and failure of hopes and dreams to materialize, we could love our broken imperfect tutors as ourselves.

After we had eaten, drunk and talked our fill, we slowly, reluctantly parted from each other's company, promising to meet up again in another six weeks. Several times, I caught Ali's eye and returned her wink. She linked her arm through mine as we got up to leave together but, Delilah, who had been hanging back with us, stopped me in my tracks.

"I can't help thinking that there's a client that you're not telling us about, Pete," she said. "There's something you're holding back!"

I felt that sharp jolt of fear and guilt in my solar plexus which came from knowing that she had found something I was keeping quiet about; that was too raw and sacred to be seen or heard.

Ali squeezed my arm and turned back, half laughing, "Well, that's for you to wonder about," she slid in lightly. "The session's over...We've closed it, remember?"

Delilah sighed as she continued to hold my gaze. "Maybe next time, huh?" she invited.

"Bye, Delilah!" I said, tuning away, surprised at the sudden sharp drumming in my chest.

We were silent as we made our way back to where our cars were parked and I knew Ali sensed that I was holding something back from the way she lingered in the silence after we had said our goodbyes. Driving home, I felt all the euphoria of the day beginning to drain away like a deflated bubble. Each time I thought about what I was holding back, I could just see Moo in my mind looking straight back at me. It bothered me that Delilah knew about Moo. On one level, it angered me because Moo wasn't a client. If anything, I was her client! She was none of Delilah's business.

Chapter Twelve

As you have your work, I have my work, and my work is dangerous,
but also of the utmost importance and it takes all my energy.
The Gospel of Moo

Around about the time of my reconnecting with the supervision group, Moo began to go missing for increasingly longer periods. When it first happened, I panicked, imagining all the worst things that could happen to her. She had got run over, jumped into someone's car and got hopelessly lost miles away from home; someone had stolen her or was holding her for ransom. I was amazed at how much Moo's disappearance disturbed me emotionally and when I checked through my list of what Moo was representing in me, I couldn't come up with anything tangible. Moo was family, my best friend even though she was a cat. Simultaneously, I couldn't help wondering if she missed me as much as I missed her. Somehow I didn't think so.

The first time Moo disappeared it was overnight and after sleepless hours tossing and turning in my bed, she appeared in the morning as if nothing had happened.

But the next time she went missing it was for almost forty-eight hours. I had already searched my neighbors' driveways and garages and was running off 'missing' posters on my computer to nail to nearby fence posts and trees.

When she returned late the second evening, her fur was all matted as if she had been neglecting herself for weeks. She looked haggard and when I picked her up, she was a lot lighter than I remembered, although this couldn't be possible. People and animals didn't lose a lot of weight in forty-eight hours. After lapping up a full bowl of milk, she yawned, stretched and disappeared to a place where she went when she really didn't want to be bothered – in between the radiator and settee. I knew better than to prod her and demand to know where she had been. She would tell me in her own time, when she was ready. And, to be quite honest, I was too afraid that my unwelcome probing would drive her away again. There was a niggling fear that she wasn't happy with me; that she had found somewhere else. Someone else. Instead, I studied her wondering and thinking that something wasn't quite right. Her warm sweet scent that had become so familiar to me, had been replaced by a metallic cold that I didn't recognize and had me worried. Impatiently, I waited for her to come to but it seemed to take hours, days before she returned to me in the way I knew her. At first she would sit on the windowsill, staring out through the glass. And when I couldn't resist touching her gently, scratching her behind her ears, which she always loved, she scarcely responded and there was no answering purr. In fact, it was as if Moo wasn't at home, as if there was just an outward husk that looked vaguely like her, but didn't smell like her or sound like her. Each time she came back to me and I could feel her presence weaving its way around me and into me like a furry caterpillar, she took longer to return. The ambience of weariness and fatigue accompanying her made me fear for her.

"What is it, Moo?" I asked, after her second journey away from me. "Are you bored and fed up with me? Is there anything I'm not giving you? Anything you need?" When she didn't answer straightaway, I voiced the fear that I held back all the time she had been away. "Have you found someone else?" I asked.

She looked at me in that authoritative way that I was used to and I swallowed uncertainty. *No*, she responded at last, *there's no one else. You are my family as I am yours. But there is something else…*Her voiced trailed off. *Something that I have to give my power and energy to…*She was sitting on my lap, facing me, but her gaze was staring past me to the window and the trees outside. *As you have your work, I have my work, and my work is dangerous, but also of the utmost importance and it takes all my energy.*

I held my breath, waiting for her to continue and when she didn't, I just reached out to stroke her. "I miss you, Moo. When you go, you leave a Moo-shaped hole."

I know. She rubbed herself against my hand.

"Would it help if I got another cat?" I didn't want another cat, but I was desperate to hang onto Moo, whatever the cost.

She met my gaze. *In a way it would, but it would have to be the right cat and I am better at finding the right cat than you.*

"I'm afraid that wherever you go, you won't come back."

Moo gave that rumbling purr in her throat that I loved so much. *I'm afraid of that too.* She sighed. *I know you want to ask me where I go, and what I do, but by letting you into that secret, I give you a responsibility. Knowledge always brings responsibility to either keep it sacred and secret, or make it public, and that might...*

"Disturb my evolution," I finished, smiling.

Moo slanted her eyes and it was as if the sun in her reached into me and touched my heart. *That's right!* She purred back, and then she began to tell me where her journeying had taken her.

When she told me that she had journeyed to that place that was held within time and space, where the Portal from the animal world to the human world had been forced open, I understood her exhaustion and the terrible sense of urgency that underscored her work.

There is so much animal cruelty in the world, Moo explained heavily. *It's getting worse, so that the animal consciousness is forcing its way into the human world without sufficient preparation. You see, very few tortured and wounded animals want to return to their animal state again. Few want to continue their evolution into human consciousness.* Moo's tail twitched. *You see, there is nothing wrong with animal consciousness and human consciousness. But when animal consciousness is wild and untamed in the case of being tortured and maddened, and then seeks to incarnate in human form before it is ready, things can take a very terrifying turn on the earth. You see, what is making its way into the human kingdom isn't wholly human or animal, it is something the Elleneron call 'Nasym' not animal, not human, just raw elemental energy which is very destructive. Nasym obstructs the flow of life. It corrupts and maims and incites terror and fear..."*

"It sounds very powerful," I said. "What can you possibly do?"

I am trying to hold the energy back by being part of a huge planetary healing process, but there aren't enough of us to cope with the inflow of Nasym entering incarnation.

"I can understand that. What will happen, Moo?"

The violence that humans have inflicted on the animal kingdom will return to them through the Nasym. Or rather, is returning through the human children coming into incarnation. They incarnate into families where their circumstances are difficult through drugs, impoverishment and lack of love which awaken the Nasym energy in them. Others incarnate into deeply privileged families who lack any moral and spiritual compass and cause mayhem within the upper classes...

"This is already happening, Moo," I murmured. "There are a lot of violent young people in our society that are terrorizing others. But Moo, the human race isn't all bad! There are many who love animals and work to release them from lives of misery and protect them and give them love like the owners of cats and dogs like your good self."

Moo gave that deep throaty sound between a purr and a meow. *If you insist on the subject of ownership, it is we who own you! We own you. Pete, surely you know you don't own me by now!* she added, her tail arching restlessly.

"Okay then, I can't disagree with that. But what I'm pointing out is the good that people do in the world, people like David Attenborough, Simon King and so many others who open awareness of the sentient beauty in all life, especially animals...Is all this wasted?"

Moo licked her paw and passed it several times over one ear. *No. The intention to protect and do good is never wasted. This is the reason why we have good people in the world who have made a comfortable transition between the animal and human world...Or else you would never have become a human.*

But, at the moment, the impulse in good people to facilitate the incarnation between animal and human levels is not high enough to outbalance the negative side. Animal cruelty far outweighs the good that is done to animals.

"What hope is there?" I asked in exasperation.

The hope is in people like you, Pete, came the swift response.

As she spoke, I was aware of a sinking feeling as if I'd known what she was going to say next.

You can help, Moo went on. *You have consciousness and awareness around what goes on for young people that are disturbed, and you also have access to the knowledge of what's happening in the evolutionary cycle. It's a knowledge that you'll probably wish you never asked for. In time...*

I knew then why Moo had chosen me. Knew that she had been right when she had said knowledge would change the way I was living my life. As all the spiritual mystics and teachers had postulated, it is harder to be conscious than unconscious.

Chapter Thirteen

The violence that humans have inflicted on the animal kingdom will return to them through the Nasym. Or rather, is returning through the human children coming into incarnation...
The Gospel of Moo

Consciousness came slowly, painfully. When it came, it brought with it the sort of bodily feelings associated with a very bad hangover: thumping headache, a tongue that felt mangled, along with an excruciating pain in my jaw and nausea. My eyes, when I opened them, felt gritty and the light was blindingly bright. My heart began to race as I became aware of the sounds around me, which quickly told me that I wasn't in my own home. Metallic, sharp sounds, lots of voices, footsteps walking hurriedly backwards and forwards and my heart skittered as I took in the sharp smell of disinfectant and alcohol.

Squinting at this bright world through puffy eyes, I slowly surveyed my situation. I was on a hospital ward. There were beds around me with patients tethered to drips of various sizes. One man opposite had tubes all over the place, draining blood out, filtering blood in and a drip stand on either side, one with a plastic pouch of blood, the other weighted down with a large bulging bag of clear fluid. On the other side of the bed was an equally bulging catheter bag of rose tinted urine that made my stomach heave. I sat up and winced as I felt a sharp resistance in my arm where, to my dismay, I too was tethered to a drip, feeding me blood like the man opposite.

"Ah, you're awake, Mr Shepherd," a young and pretty blonde haired nurse suddenly appeared beside me, beaming brightly. "I'm Sally...And I'm looking after you today."

I tried to speak but my tongue felt thick and unwieldy as if I had come out of the dentist after a filling.

The nurse smiled. "It'll be a bit difficult to speak at the moment because you've had a few stitches in your tongue and it'll be a little while before the swelling goes down. The tongue bleeds quite a bit so that's why we've put you on a drip. Also we've had to put plates in your jaw to hold the broken bone in place..." My heart missed a beat as I squawked a word at her. The smiling nurse adjusted the blood pressure cuff on my arm and I felt it tighten. "Just checking your obs," she explained. "You also broke your lower left arm, so we've set that and plastered it."

I squawked again in an effort to know what had happened to me.

"I suppose you don't remember how you got here," she said, her face concerned.

I shook my head vigorously and then wished I hadn't as I winced at the pain in my neck.

"You were brought into Accident and Emergency last night. A neighbor had heard a lot of shouting outside his house and found a group of drunken youths outside who ran off when they saw him. Luckily, he found you. Apparently, you were lying in the road semi-conscious. The police called to see how you were and said they would be around later today to see if you're up to answering any questions." She smiled, as she unhooked the cuff. "Your obs are fine, so in a couple of days, all being well, you'll be ready to go home...Do you remember anything about what happened?"

There was something dark in my mind, lurking there like the remnants of a bad dream, but the content was splintered and incomplete. Something about stones hitting a metallic surface outside my window...And then the memories petered out.

I shrugged this time and found even that painful. Sally handed me a plain white notepad and a pen. "Use that. Do you have next of kin?"

I thought of Moo and the sudden sharp pain in my chest as I

did so almost winded me. I moved my head carefully from side to side

"Girlfriend? Friend? Neighbor?"

Ali? I dismissed her briefly. But then backtracked, remembering how she had made me promise that I should contact her if I got into trouble with my medication or hit a bad space. I was also thinking of Moo. Who would feed her if I weren't there?

I began, shakily, writing Ali's name on the notepad, scribbling a question mark next to her phone number and writing 'Buttercup farm… Linden.' I handed it back to Sally who folded it, placing it carefully in the pocket of her tunic.

"Okay, that's great! I'll leave a message if I can't speak to her directly." She hesitated before turning away. "Are you on any medication? I noticed from your notes that you suffer from Bipolar Disorder."

'I'm on Lithium,' I scribbled on the notepad.

"We need to get you prescribed for that…I'll get a Psyche up to see you," she smiled, noticing how exhausted I was as I sank back against the pillow. "The best you can do in the meantime is get as much rest as you can."

I tried to fight the treacly tide of exhaustion I had been holding at bay, but moments later I collapsed back against the pillow, as unconsciousness claimed me. Almost immediately, I fell into a troubled dream where four hooded youths had me surrounded and were pushing me about from one to the other, taking it in turns to land me a punch. In the dream, I lashed out fiercely my fists making contact with flesh, but then everything went blank, as I was steadily outnumbered. The last thing I remember was one of the youths with a strong Glaswegian accent leering over me, his stale beery breath in my face. His hood fell back briefly and I saw that he wore a gold ring in his left nostril, his spiky bleached hair was dark at the roots and his earlobe bore the swastika tattoo.

Much later, after I awoke again, I was able to pass on these details to the police who came and asked me questions.

Over the next twenty-four hours I floated in and out of consciousness as my body struggled to heal itself. At one time I woke up in the night with the sense that I was burning up and called out hoarsely, my tongue throbbing painfully, as a nurse I didn't recognize put another drip up, this time a small pocket of pale yellow fluid. "We're giving you some antibiotics intravenously," the nurse explained. "You're running a temperature..." I pointed to my mouth. "I know, she conceded. "Your mouth's dry... I'm afraid we're giving you all the fluids you need intravenously for now. We don't want you vomiting with that jaw."

After that, I drifted in and out of sleep plagued by disturbing dreams of my past, of Moo and flashbacks from the street fight the other night. My first thought when I touched consciousness was Moo. Where was she? How was she? She was my real next of kin. Why couldn't she be with me now? Supposing something had happened to her and I hadn't been around to look after her? Supposing she was lying somewhere injured? The thought was unbearable and I blanked it out.

But then, after drifting off for another few hours, I would jerk to, adrenalin coursing through me. Where was Moo when I needed her? And then, a little later; for that matter, where was I when Moo needed me?

In retrospect, I could see I had become far too involved with Moo and her frequent disappearances. As a result, I had neglected my own physical needs and state of emotional and mental health. But the more I had allowed myself to be pulled into the fantastic dynamics of her world, the more I had begun to depend on Moo for my emotional stability – except her disappearances were making me more and more emotionally unstable.

At first I hadn't noticed that I wasn't sleeping more than a couple of hours a night, after which I was wide awake, up listening to music, watching videos, on the internet and then going jogging in the morning before my first client arrived and hoping and hoping that Moo would have arrived back from her travels before I got back. My behavior was typically manic, impossibly euphoric, electrically wired, plugged into the mains feeling. I was so high that I didn't know I was high!

Somehow the 'higher' I became, the less easy it was to monitor myself. It was always easy when I was depressed, as the isolation of that was so unbearable that it forced me to check out my lithium levels.

Over the last couple of weeks, prior to landing in hospital, I had felt mildly euphoric, weller-than-well. But then my body became uncomfortable to be in. I began pacing endlessly from room to room, cramped by the spatial limitations of the flat; two bedrooms, Lilliputian lounge, kitchen and conservatory that was too cold in winter and impossibly hot in summer.

It was the pacing that made me realize I was high, but not a comfortable high. It was as if I had fire ants under my skin, making it impossible to remain still or quiet for any length of time. Somehow, I had always managed to maintain my work with clients, up until it got too bad. But then I had to cancel them which I hated doing, knowing how disruptive this could be to a therapeutic alliance. A supervision group had come and gone and I had glanced through their papers without commenting on them or sending them anything of my own. What could I say? The fact was that my whole life had come to revolve around a cat who could talk and who disappeared for long periods of a time in an effort to mend the damage we had wreaked on the animal kingdom? Even in my, then, mildly euphoric state, I could see how whacky this sounded to outsiders...

In the hospital bed, I drifted in and out of consciousness so much that I no longer knew whether I was dreaming or not. Distantly, I was aware of the night light over my bed flashing on as a nurse came to attend me, felt the cuff tightening on my arm, the cool invasion of the tympanic probe in my ear and the sharp bite of a needle in my arm as some painkiller was administered. What had begun as mild discomfort in my bladder was getting worse as I tried again to use the hospital cardboard bottle without success. Later, I flinched as cold lubricating gel was smeared over my lower abdomen and the even colder sensation of the bladder scan probe on top of that. Then, to my horror, I had to endure being catheterized in the early hours of the morning because my bladder had gone into retention. It didn't help that a nurse explained that retention happened as a reaction to various drugs, together with the anesthetic and that this would only be temporary. But, to my relief, the sharp dragging pain in my bladder had gone, allowing me to relax. It wasn't only the indignity of being catheterized, it was the thought that I was wired up to so many devices that I couldn't make an easy escape.

Day rolled into night. Day began early. Too early, with the buzz of nurses chatting excitedly at the ward station as the shift changed. The obs and drug rounds followed where everything about my bodily functions were recorded and monitored with the precision of a car undergoing its annual servicing. My new name was 'Bed 7' and there was more interest in my fluid input and output chart than anyone had showed me in my entire life.

The room was bathed in sunlight when I next became aware of anything. I lay there for a while, soaking up the peace that seemed to envelope me. All the knotted bits in my mind seemed to unravel and become relaxed as my breathing slowed.

Moo...

I knew she was around. I could feel her. That sort of fine tickling of zillions of electrical frissons zipping up, and through, my body. As my mind relaxed I felt my consciousness that had been compressed into a tight golf ball, slowly become released unravel, stretching out, and out...

Moo?

I'm here...

I held my breath as her purr seemed to enter my being.

"Where Moo?" I heard myself ask. Because my tongue was still too swollen and sore to be able to articulate anything verbally, I thought it at her.

At last, I heard her respond diplomatically; *you're learning to speak with your mind rather than your tongue...It's a much more efficient way of communication because your tongue can say one thing and your mind another.*

I smiled inwardly at a light pressure on my chest. And now I could see her through my closed eyelids. The daylight that was in the room was her own incandescence, that special light she brought with her.

"Are you all right?" I questioned mentally. "Where have you been? Are you hungry?" the questions rushed in.

By reply, her calm answered me, saturating any troubled areas of my being.

But then Moo gave that wonderful inner smile as she returned my gaze. It was as if I was all lit up inside, as though a great sunbeam had swept into a dusty darkened room. *I'm never far away. I'll never leave you...*

Tears pricked my eyes as she spoke, and I didn't care.

"Where have you been?" I asked, but I didn't need to ask. I knew. She had been in that place which took all her energy as she tried to hold back the dark energy, which was, inexorably, sweeping across the psychic template of the earth. She had once explained it to me in more technical scientific terms; why the electromagnetic energy of the field was changing and the effect that this change was having on young people whose physiological systems were not fully developed.

Well, I heard her think. *You've got yourself into a right state.*

"I know," I thought back.

What happened? she asked.

I looked at her surprised, taken aback by her ignorance. Up until then I assumed Moo knew everything.

*Of course I know what happened to you. I'm just wondering if **you** know what happened to you.*

"I was attacked," I thought back. "I went out because I heard kids throwing stones."

And how were you feeling before you went out to them?

I hesitated, "I was high...agitated, restless...Why?"

Do you think they were normal kids? Moo continued to probe.

"Normal?" I thought back indignantly. What d'you mean? They were drunk and..."

My words trailed off as I remembered what Moo had told me about those who were neither animal nor wholly human entering incarnation. What had she called them, the Nasym?

Moo smiled again into my soul and I experienced it as a child would with a rewarding smile from an attentive parent.

They were drawn to your energy.

"Because I was high?"

Partly...When you're high you tend to beam out a lot of bright excited energy and those that are impregnated with dark energy are drawn to it even though it hurts them too. You remember why I said I had chosen you...

"Yes, I do...."

The warm pressure on my chest spread to my limbs, my hands and feet and, gratefully, the rest of me fell into this healing pool of oblivion.

Chapter Fourteen

The peace and well-being I had experienced with Moo stayed with me until the morning or, rather, when the hospital staff regarded morning to be. Despite the drawn curtains and fluorescent lights, I could see that it was still dark outside the window.

Sally, bright as ever, checked my obs and gave her approval. "Well, the good news is your temperature's down so the antibiotics must have kicked in..." she glanced at me as she made a note on my chart. "How's the pain?"

'Okay,' I scribbled on the pad. 'Until I try to speak.'

"At least you're managing to," she smiled. She handed me some iced water with a straw. "Try taking sips of this," she offered, adding, "Careful...Sips I said," as I grabbed the plastic cup eagerly. "It's mainly to refresh your mouth. You're still up for IV fluids..." She tilted her head sideways questioningly. "How'd you fancy getting up for a wash today?"

I scanned myself in dismay, noting that there were no fewer bags and tubes attached to me than previously.

"We can wheel you to the bathroom," she offered brightly. "It'll do you good to move around a bit. It gets your circulation going."

Never let it be said that hospital is a place to rest and recuperate. Following a very clumsy wash, after which I did actually feel better, I was visited by the surgical registrar and his team, all who despite my own personal shortcomings, seemed to think I would be ready for discharge in ten days times which was both good and frightening. How would I cope? Who would feed Moo while I was here? I had to find someone.

The moment the registrar and his team had given their prognosis and moved on to complete the round, a psychiatrist, Richard Wysnieski, appeared at my side, sporting a Freudian beard and looking closer to his sell-by-date than I did with his bloodshot eyes and pale complexion. "I'm writing you up for Lithium," he said, pen poised over my drug chart. "How is your mental and emotional state now?"

I hesitated briefly, thinking of how I'd been before Moo's visit. 'Okay,' I signed with my working hand. His pen hovered as he studied me over his glasses. "How were you before your accident? High? Low? Normal?"

God! What the hell was normal?

He was studying me over the rim of his glasses and I remember thinking how well he fitted the stereotypical psychiatrist from the late 1960s, round about the time when all psychologists were uniformed in their tank tops.

'High!' I indicated wildly and continued to scribble on the pad. 'At least high enough to take on those kids and land myself here!'

His pen hovered in his notes. "Did anything in particular make you high? An emotional upset?"

Moo...Moo had been missing for too long.

'I think it was seasonal,' I scribbled.

He nodded and skewed a glance at his watch and I had a mental image of him having to traipse along to more medical wards, from hospital to hospital, where a lot of the failed suicides were admitted, and having to see eight other patients before lunch. To him, I was just one of many, a statistic in his book. "Is there anything else I can do for you?"

I shook my head forgetting, and winced.

He hesitated before moving away. "I've had a word with Jenny Doyle, the social worker...She should be up to see you later this morning. She's just a bit concerned about you living on your own and not having anyone to care for you after discharge. You don't seem to need further hospitalization for your mental condition," he added, scratching his beard as he mused aloud. "But there's a concern that you might end up in the same space as before – going high again – which isn't good after the injuries you've had. You might feel that you can do more than you think you can..." He hummed to himself tunelessly, before finally offering: "Perhaps you could pop into the outpatient clinic for a few weeks after discharge so we can keep you monitored."

I resisted wearing the straitjacket of a grounded teenager and met him halfway; scribbling on the pad. 'Doesn't look like I'll be going home straight away...Maybe you can pop round this time next week, just before I go home.'

He nodded and made a note of it.

I'd just managed a few sips of lukewarm coffee and was on the point of sinking into the sudden exhaustion that seemed to claim me after the slightest effort, when Jenny Doyle arrived, a trim attractive woman in her mid thirties with natural chestnut brown hair framing her face in that popular Victoria Beckham bob.

"I've just had a word with the Psyche," she began after the initial introductions, "and he seems to think you're emotionally strong enough to cope at home on your own – but we both agree that it would be good if you had someone with you, a neighbor or friend who could be around in the first couple of weeks after discharge." She flashed me a warm smile. "This is purely for practical reasons...You'll have one arm in plaster and even if you manage to find a take-away meal within walking distance, it'll be hard work with a broken jaw and notepad to make yourself understood, and it'll be a while before you can drive, of course."

I was stung by my own sense of growing helplessness and loss of autonomy. I had, without any consideration, thought that I would be able to drive around still, but it would be a few more weeks after discharge before this was possible. Correction: legally possible.

'What do you suggest?' I wrote, 'Meals-on-wheels?' She returned my wry smile. "I think we can both agree that that won't be a workable solution...This friend of yours, Ali Buttercup, in Linden. We've tried ringing a few times, but no reply...We've left messages to contact us as soon as she gets the message."

I shrugged. "Half term!" I scribbled. "She's probably away with her son."

"Do you have a mobile number for her?" Jenny suggested.

'Not on me,' I responded honestly. 'I have a cat to look after,' I added. 'She'll need feeding. She probably hasn't eaten for three days. I know cats are resilient, but she still needs someone to look after her.'

The social worker was scribbling down notes. "We can arrange for someone to go in and feed her, but I doubt whether I can get anyone before tomorrow." She smiled. "Well, so far, we've managed to find a solution for your cat...But not for you. I'm not happy sending you home on your own."

I was getting tired and irritable and stressed about Moo. She might run away, find someone else, and yet, when we had communicated last night, she had seemed well and happy and told me not to worry.

Seeing how tired I was, Jenny promised she would try and arrange for a clinical support worker to come in at least once a day, while I was rehabilitating, to help me with meals, do any shopping I needed and pick up medicines. She would make a few further phone calls and would pick up from where we had left off afterwards. Vaguely, I was aware of thanking her and then must have sunk into the tide of exhaustion because then I was dreaming that I was back in time, playing basketball with a colleague from University and whose name I'd forgotten.

Consciousness returned in the warm sensual fragrance of patchouli and rose, a soft hand in mine while another stroked my brow. For a while, I lay there, not wanting to stir for fear of disturbing the clear image I had in my mind of Ali. In the middle distance were the busy sounds of trays being lifted out of the meal trolley, nurses and clinical workers hurrying backwards and forwards and the smell of boiled vegetables and meat.

"Pete..." Ali's voice now, close to my ear, the smell of her warm spicy breath. "Are you in there?"

My grin was a grimace as I opened heavy eyelids.

She touched a finger to my lips as I tried to respond, wincing as I did so. "Don't speak," she grinned down at me. "That way I can be in control...And you know how I love that."

I bit back spontaneous laughter because the movement hurt.

"I daren't touch you," she said. "Is there anywhere that doesn't hurt or isn't wired up?"

I winked at her and she grinned, "I don't think that's strictly legal in here," she glanced down at the catheter bag, "or would do much for you or at the moment?"

I reached for the pad and pen and began scribbling. 'How are you?'

"Fine...And yes, the hospital rang me, but I had tried contacting you anyway because I was worried." She wound a strand of hair round her fingers as she always did when she was wondering how to say something. 'Cut the crap,' I wanted to scribble, 'cut to the chase.' But I deliberately held back, knowing that of all the people I knew, Ali was the least likely one to prevaricate over embarrassing or important issues. I had always admired her ability to articulate her feelings and get to the point.

"You see, I had a very vivid dream last night," she began, winding a strand of hair as tight as it would go round her finger so its tip went bright red. "I dreamt of a cat. Well, it was a very vivid dream and the cat, sort of spoke to me."

I swallowed, aware of my accelerated heart rate and the sheer frustration of not being able to respond verbally. All I could do by way of response was grunt encouragement.

"Well, I know you mentioned having a cat – and that may have influenced the dream in some way...But I don't know what your cat looks like...Anyway this one was all black, a ball of black fur with the cutest green eyes I have ever seen."

'What did she say?' I wrote.

She checked my face for signs of disbelief saw none and went on. "She said she was worried about you because you had had an accident and were in hospital...She said her name was 'Moo'," she chuckled. "Sounds like a cow."

Stifling a relieved grin was one of the hardest things I had to do and I groaned as I felt the added tension in my jaw. 'That's my cat's name...Moo!'

We stared at each other then down at the pad where I wrote in a shaky hand. 'Then what?'

"Well, Patrick and I were staying at our holiday caravan in Wales for a long weekend when I had the dream...One of the reasons I'd taken him there was because we lost Molly – remember the elderly tabby, she died of leukemia last week and he was really cut up about it."

Unable to hold myself back any more, I wrote, 'I'm sorry about that, but did Moo say anything else?'

She frowned "Not that I can remember...She just asked me if I could go and visit you." She smiled. "But I would have come anyway," she tutted. "Who did this to you? You look awful, Pete!"

I shrugged and wrote 'Drunken kids...'

"You look as if you've stepped out of a boxing ring."

'Yeah, I had a look for the first time this morning,' I wrote.

She took my hand and squeezed it. "You know they're not going to let you go unless you have someone to keep an eye on you, don't you?"

I thought of Moo. She would keep an eye on me, but somehow that didn't help.

'I need someone to feed Moo while I'm in here.'

"I know, and I've been thinking...How about you and Moo coming to stay with us at the farm for a while? Patrick's okay about it and I know he will be happy to have a male adult figure around. In fact, he would be thrilled."

An instinctive arch of my eyebrows sent sharp pain into my nose and I wrote, 'You don't have to do this?'

"No, I don't…But honestly, Pete, practically, what choice have you got?" She pursed her lips, "Of course, you could self-discharge, but you and I know enough about the system to understand that if the psyche and social worker between them think you're not fit to go home, they'll prolong your discharge by having you admitted to a locked ward at Rylands until you *are* fit to go," she sighed, "and your cat, Moo would have to go into a cattery until you were discharged…That's six weeks in a place she doesn't want to be, and what I understand from her is that's she's an intelligent cat…"

'OK,' I agreed in large capital letters on a fresh sheet of paper. 'You've made your point!'

"Pete," Ali rolled her eyes. "It's not a question of scoring points, winning or losing, I'm just thinking of the best deal for both of us. To put it bluntly, I'd like having you around for a while, it's not because I'm feeling sorry for you. If I feel sorry for anyone it's Moo – although I don't even know her and imagine she's quite capable of looking after herself anyway. You'd have your own room, and Patrick would certainly like having Moo around even if you're not that impressed…"

I grabbed her hand and wrote, 'thanks, I'm convinced. I'd love it, you're my guardian angel.'

"Guardian, I might be, "she grinned, "but angel I'm not, as you'll soon have the pleasure of finding out."

With that agreement and a simultaneous surrender of any male emotional baggage of being independent, strong and magnanimous, rather than reduced, dependant and pathetically helpless, I allowed a sense of rightness to sweep in. I intuitively sensed that despite everything that had happened to me, there was something intrinsically right about it at the same time. It was as if the universe had conspired to make this possible, or rather Moo had tapped into her blessed 'Mooisphere' and created a need that held possibility and a solution at the same time. It wasn't as if Ali was a stranger. We had endured the grueling agony of the Foundation Year in our psychotherapy training together with her parental alienation and my absent father and ill mother, and we had emerged wounded but strong in the broken places.

'I wonder when they'll let me go?'

"Leave it with me. I'll go and talk to someone and see if we can't make it a lot sooner than predicted."

She went up to the desk before I could stop her and after a few minutes the Ward Manager who'd just begun her shift came and sat beside me, asking me all the questions I expected her to ask; Was I comfortable with staying with Ali? How long had we known each other?

When I told her about the training we had done together and our long friendship, I saw her visibly relax and pat my arm. "That sounds the best possible solution for you, Mr Shepherd. The main thing is that your friend is aware of your bipolar disorder as well as your injuries, which will soon heal...I've just spoken to her," she smiled. "And she seems like a friend worth having."

'She is...' I wrote. 'So when can I go?'

"We'd like you to stay for a few more days just to make sure that infection of yours has cleared up properly and there are no more bleeds which would signify underlying damage that the X rays might not have picked up...If everything's okay and we can take the catheter out without any problems, then there's no reason why you shouldn't be able to leave on the condition you have a Community Nurse to redress your wounds each day and monitor your progress...How are you feeling emotionally?" she asked, referring to my bipolar disorder.

I signaled a 'thumbs up' to her and she smiled before excusing herself to answer her bleep.

Surrendering my flat keys to Ali so that she could look in on Moo, I made her promise to ring me and let me know whether she was there and, if she was, how she was. Moo was my only worry now.

About an hour later one of the nurses brought a portable phone up to me. "There's a call for you, Mr Shepherd, from a friend."

"Well, Moo is here!" came Ali's triumphant voice. "She was waiting by the door as if she was expecting me. Right now, she's on my lap, purring..."

I wanted to ask her if she looked poorly, had lost weight and was hungry but could only groan an acknowledgement.

"She was hungry but she doesn't look too bad. She's probably found someone else to feed her or give her a saucer of milk while you've been away. Cats always have foster homes they can rely on if problems hit their home ground," her voice came again. "I gave another inane acknowledging grunt, "If you wait a moment," came Ali's voice, "you might be able to hear her purr."

I felt any residual tension drain away as I listened to Moo's unmistakable throaty purr.

"Mmmm," I grunted, glad that I couldn't articulate much more because I suddenly felt emotionally overwhelmed.

"Anyway, I'll stay with Moo a little longer and put enough dry food down for tomorrow and I'll look in on her once a day until you're ready to leave the hospital."

There was a pause and the sound of rustling papers in the background. "There's a load of mail here for you – and I'll bring that in for you tomorrow...Oh, and there were several messages on the answer phone... one from someone called Kevin who wanted to see you because he got into Veterinary School in Liverpool, probably one of your clients..."

When I replaced the receiver several tears plopped onto my plastered arm and I brushed them away uncaring of what I looked like. Kevin's success, Ali's generosity, Moo being safe and cared for – it was all too much.

But, much more than this were the reasons behind Kevin wanting to become a vet instead of a more glamorous and artistic career in photography. He had confided in me, once when we met up, that the reason he'd had a breakdown was because he was betraying himself. He knew that working with animals was his vocation. He knew this because Moo had visited him and told him that his skills were needed in communicating with the animals and, especially those raw animal beings trapped in human bodies in the form of the Nasym. No one understood the Nasym more than one who had been one himself while he was trying to find relief in drugs. Once he had made this decision to become a vet, the soul sickness in him had gone.

Chapter Fifteen

'Reason' I don't understand because it's manmade. But 'purpose' I can understand. And she began to purr. *Purpose unites and inspires individual work to the common good of all...*
The Gospel of Moo

After Ali's visit, all the taut strands of elastic that seemed to be holding me together began to relax, become unfettered, so that I felt like a filleted fish. Instead of an uncertain present, tipping into some dark and sinister future where I feared for Moo and myself, a vista of hope and expectation lay ahead of me. I felt the gratitude and sense of relief of a soldier returning from the Front. And this new injection of hope and promise seemed to allow any true healing to take place. If I lay there and closed my eyes, I could almost feel my body healing, the bone matrix in my arm knitting back together again as osteoblasts formed. The stitches were beginning to dissolve in my tongue and when I moved it the pain had given way to an uncomfortable tightness rather than a sharp pain. My mouth still felt as though it was stuffed with a gritty sponge but I marveled at the body's ability to regenerate so quickly. Yet, emotional and mental stability, driven by a more obscure neuronal, ancestral and historical processes lagged far behind. Although my jaw still ached, it was a healthy ache rather than one that held unbearable fragility. The stale urine smell when the catheter bags were emptied each night no longer belonged to me. I could move my left arm freely without the sharp sting of the cannula testing the vein where IV fluids entered my body.

When I slept now, whether it was night or day, I sank into a deep pile of living breathing warmth, which I could only describe as fur. Fur that neither stifled nor suffocated but, instead, seemed to cocoon and envelop me as though I was a baby. I dreamt of

Moo. Dreamt that she was huge: a big cat with paws that padded silently through night and day unseen. Ever padding, rarely stopping for rest, for she was driven by purpose and aligned to a destination I could not know. Cocooned in her soft honeyed warmth, I dreamt that I was being carried in her belly, in her womb.

This was my living crucible of healing. I would be reborn new, changed and stronger than ever before. This I knew. This I believed.

Ali came to visit me on several more occasions. Once when I was asleep after a long morning of physiotherapy. I was surprised at how much three weeks of inactivity compromised muscle tone. I was genuinely shocked at how weak and shaky I felt as I pushed simple weights with my legs and lifted what I thought was my good arm.

"Don't worry too much," the Physio pressed. "Your strength will all come back. Muscle tone vanishes quickly, but it also builds up quickly as well. Don't forget you've suffered a psychological shock as well as a very real physical one. Parts of the body we normally take for granted close down as energy is diverted to regenerating bruised and broken tissue and bone."

"Do you know what happened to me?" I questioned painfully, testing my speech now.

"It was in the local paper as well as in your notes," she explained. "Made the front page... It would be hard to miss."

"Do you know if they were caught, the kids that did it?"

She shook her head, "I just read about the police having a gang of youths in for questioning, nothing more." She handed me a peak flow meter. "Just blow as hard as you can into that." Awkwardly, painfully, I did as instructed and handed it back to her. "That's fine," she said. "There's nothing wrong with your lungs. It's just your muscle tone that needs working on...I'll schedule another appointment when you're discharged to get your arm working once you have your plaster removed. At least with simple injuries like yours, it's just a matter of time and persistence."

The second time Ali visited I was up, dressed and sitting in the television room watching *Match of the Day*.

"Alright for some," she grinned as she sat down beside me, brushing her lips against my cheek and I caught the familiar scent of patchouli tempered with rose. "Watching television all day, while the rest of us are slaving away in the fields!"

I gave her a playful punch. "I'm bored senseless, Ali...You can change places with me any day and I'll take my turn tilling the fields with pleasure."

"You're speaking!" she exclaimed. "And you look heaps better," she observed, brightly. "You just need to put some weight on.

"That shouldn't be too hard with Patrick's cooking!" I said, deliberately holding back from asking how Moo was. "Also don't make me laugh, please. It hurts like hell, still!"

"I'll do my best. But, ever since Patrick knew that you were coming to stay, he has been baking cakes, making bread and been on at me to shop for more ingredients so that he can expand his cuisine to fit in the freezer!"

"Brilliant...Much as I have no reason to complain about the hospital food, as it isn't bad considering it's cooked in bulk, it does get very predictable after a while. You know, fish and chips on Friday, a choice of Hotpot on Thursday or cheese lasagna or chicken sandwich, trifle for sweet..... And I'm pig sick of pureed food with this wretched jaw."

"What do you really long for?" Ali asked.

"I long for..." I sighed and closed my eyes. "I long for fresh air, the feel of the wind and rain against my skin...The sight of blossom whirling down from the trees...Red and white candles on the chestnut trees....Swallows and swifts screaming through the skies." *And you in my arms*, I thought, before I could stop myself.

Ali smiled, squeezing my arm. "Well, I can't cook, but I can promise you all of that."

"How's Moo?" I tried, almost tentatively.

I took her momentary hesitation as a bad sign and was alarmed at how rapidly my thoughts nosedived into chaos...Something had happened to Moo. She had run away, got lost, run over. My breathing quickened as I realized how much Moo had become my anchor.

"She's fine, absolutely fine," Ali replied. "She's very settled in!"

I stared at her uncomprehendingly. "Settled in?"

Ali sighed. "She moved in with us a few days ago...I decided after the first visit that she wanted to have company, and she has taken to the farm like a fish to water.

My surprised look dissolved into a huge grin. "Oh wonderful!" I grasped her hands. "I'm so glad. Moo needs company."

"*And*...she paid her rent the first day. Three mice laid outside the backdoor in a neat line."

We both laughed, and although it was painful to do this, I didn't care. "I don't know how to thank you."

She smiled, her almond shaped eyes twinkling mischievously. "Don't worry, I'll find a way. But the main thing is you begin to build your strength up when you get to the farm...Go on those long walks you've been craving. What's the Doc or Psyche said?"

"I'm going for an X- ray tomorrow, and if my jaw's healing up okay, I should be able to come home – come to yours tomorrow."

Ali squeezed my hand "I prefer the sound of 'home'," she said, handing me a brown bag. "These are from Pat. He made me promise that I would give them to you."

I had a peek at them and my mouth watered as the sweet warm scent tantalized my senses. "Rock cakes! I love rock cakes! Takes me back to my childhood when Mum used to make them every weekend. No one ever makes them these days."

She smiled. "I did tell him that they weren't the ideal thing for a broken jaw, but they are a lot softer than they sound." She stood up. "I have to get back to pick Pat up from school," she said. "He's so excited. It's his birthday on Saturday and he wants you to be here by then."

"His tenth?"

"Yes."

"Can you get him something from me – but only if you let me pay for it."

"Done," she said. "He needs a new football as the other one got waterlogged in the stream."

"What have you got him?"

She grinned. "You'll have to come and see for yourself...Just get better."

"Give my love to Moo, won't you?"

"Will do," she said, as she was leaving. "She likes tuna, doesn't she?"

"Tell me about it!" As she walked away, the changing air currents wafted the scent of patchouli and rose in my direction. For a long time the scent lingered in the air.

Now, it seemed that I had fur growing on the inside of me, smoothing out all the raw and exposed places. It was as if I were carrying Moo inside my belly too.

I must have dozed off watching *Match of the Day*, because when I came to, I was aware of someone sitting next to me. It was a gaunt middle-aged man dressed in hospital issue mandarin colored pajamas. At first when I looked at him, I thought he'd been holidaying out in the sun, until I realized the golden tan was more yellow in color. He was, in fact, yellow from the roots of his hair to his hands. Bright yellow! Even his eyes were yellow, the irises pale orange.

The yellow man extended his yellow hand unsteadily. "Terry," he introduced himself. "Was it a good match?"

"Pete," I responded, taking his hand. "Well, it was until I fell asleep."

We both laughed and the sudden sharp pain in my jaw made me laugh more because laughing felt so good.

"How long have you been in here?" he asked.

I shrugged. "To tell you the truth, I've lost all sense of time…I think it must be two or three weeks, but it honestly feels like months."

"I know, time is such a strange thing…"

"What are you in for?" I asked. "You look a bit yellow."

"Jaundiced is the medical term," Terry explained, "which is another word for canary yellow!" We both laughed. "Did you know that you have a black cat sitting round your shoulders?"

"A what?"

"Black cat. She's as clear as day. A longhaired one at that…" The man started coughing and I noticed flecks of blood on his handkerchief.

"Are you all right, mate?"

"Yep," he cleared his throat and I heard the rattle of phlegm.

"She'll never leave you, that cat," he said. "One day you'll think she has left you – but it'll only be for a very short while, and then she'll be back again – stronger than ever."

A couple of years ago I would have ridiculed what this patient had said, putting it down to hallucinations or an imbalanced mind. But I had experienced so much since Moo had come into my life that I wasn't as easily fazed by the unusual or whacky.

"Well – gotta go," Terry said, shuffling away. He held out his hand again. "Pleased to meet you and – your cat!"

"Hey mate!" I called after him. "What ward are you on?"

He hesitated, his yellow gaze holding mine. "To tell you the truth, mate, I've forgotten. I've been on so many…" He jabbed his thumb up the corridor. "It's eight, seven, thirteen or twelve. Take your pick! It's on the medical floor anyway. Wards are all the same to me…Bye mate."

"Bye…"

For a while the yellow man who had seen Moo so clearly around my shoulders, as she often sat, stayed in my mind. There was something hauntingly memorable about him, not just because he was the first yellow man I had seen, but because there was a sadness about him, a loneliness. I don't know what I thought I could do for him. He was obviously ill, but somehow because he had seen Moo it created an invisible bond between us.

The next day after my morning X-ray, I was given the all clear. I was due to be discharged the next day and my care package would start then, twice weekly visits from the district nurse, weekly physiotherapy and a week or so after that, my plaster would be removed. In the early days of my injuries, when every muscle and bone in my body seemed to ache, I thought I would never heal, never be able to walk away from the oppressive hospital smells or the bed that I seemed immured in.

About an hour before Ali was due to come and collect me, I remembered Terry and decided to go in search of him to wish him well and thank him for telling me about Moo. I had been too surprised to thank him, or confirm that what he had said was true, or even applied to me.

What ward did he say he was on? One of the medical wards, was it? They were all on the same floor, so surely all I needed to do was ask around. All the same, putting it into perspective, apart from my own ward there were still five other thirty-six bedded wards that he could have got swallowed up in. The only discerning feature was that he was yellow. Except, he wasn't the only yellow or rather, jaundiced person I had seen around. There were others, fully mobile, pushing drip stands or catheter plastic hangers around like modern day accessories.

I was hovering about on the landing trying to rustle up the courage to enter a strange ward and become engulfed in its own unique biosphere when a male nurse met me with a friendly smile. "Lost?" he asked.

"I'm looking for someone, a patient who came to see me yesterday..."

"Can you remember the ward he was on?"

"No...I don't think he knew himself...Said he was on a medical ward though."

"Did he give his name? You said he was mobile?"

"Yes, he was mobile...His name was Terry and he was...er, yellow..."

The young man smiled easily. "Oh – I think I know who you mean...He was on ward seven, my ward, the day before yesterday...But he might have been moved...I'll find out for you."

I waited at the end of the corridor watching the activity around me. There were patients in varying states of dress and undress being wheeled from the ward and into the lift. The metal doors swung backwards and forwards as beds carrying patients, accompanied by clinical staff holding drip stands and oxygen cylinders disappeared and reappeared. Patients loitered about on the landing looking lost while others hung round the frozen drinks machine or gazed out at the view across the rooftops. Other patients appeared from the lifts smelling of cigarette smoke, either smartly dressed or wearing hospital issue nightwear. There was one obese patient sitting in a wheelchair wearing a hospital issue operation gown, rolls of pastry colored skin showing through the undone ties. A skull and crossbones lay partially visible at the neck where the black dyed hair was parted. She was whispering loudly to another equally obese patient standing at her side wearing pink baby dolls with 'Princess' in gold scrawled across large ample boobs. Her arms were covered in tattoos of cartoon characters and a gothic coffin one across her right wrist. Everyone stopped to stare as a huge patient dressed in a theatre gown, which hung half open at the back revealed leather black thongs every third step. What passed for normal here would be regarded as indecent dress anywhere else. Harassed relatives clung together in tight clusters in ward corridors speaking sharply to each other, staring suspiciously at staff members as they walked by as if they were potential abusers of their confused relative.

A battalion of cleaners caught my attention; dressed in striped mauve and white tunic and pants, pushing cleaning stands of mops, buckets, refuse bags and cloths towards each of the ward entrances, wiping their hands with alcohol gel as they entered. If MRSA or Clostridium Difficile lurked in the corners of the wards, they had to go into hiding if they were to survive. Theatre technicians wandered back and forth, their hair concealed by green hats as they chauffeured patients to and from theatre. Nurses laughed and exchanged words as they began and ended their shifts. One nurse hurried across the forecourt with an ECG machine up the corridor and into the clamor of patient bells, all vying for the attention of the meager staff available.

Eventually, the male nurse returned looking a little puzzled. "If it's the same Terry I know, he took a turn for the worse yesterday, and was admitted to HDU." He stopped. "Did he have two silver earrings in his left ear?"

"Yes...Yes, he did."

"Well he had a Cardiac Arrest this morning," he frowned. "He couldn't have come to see you actually, he wouldn't have been able to...He was unconscious."

"But he did..."

"I think you must have got him confused with someone else."

I nodded, something catching in my throat because I knew deep down. I knew that it was the same Terry who had come to see me and shaken my hand, and told me about Moo. I don't know how I knew...I just knew.

"He was an alcoholic wasn't he...This Terry?" The words tumbled out of me.

The nurse seemed less sure now. "We're not really meant to

give out that sort of information to anyone other than friends and relatives."

I wanted to say: *but he didn't have any friends or relatives, did he?* Because they had all disowned him. Instead, I thanked him and moved back up the corridor, towards my ward to pick up my things and wait for Ali's arrival, towards the new life that would be waiting for me.

Standing outside the hospital, wearing jogging pants and trainers, I closed my eyes to slow down the euphoric rush of visual, olfactory and tactile impressions that hit my senses. I felt like a horse that had been enclosed in a stable for too long, cantering out to meet the explosive rush of impressions leaving me reeling and gasping for breath. I don't think I have ever felt so grateful to be alive and free as I did then.

Ali honked the horn. "Come on," she urged. "You'll catch your death out there."

With a bodily reluctance, I slipped into the Range Rover and returned the broad grin that Patrick flashed at me as he sat in the back, his hands fidgeting excitedly. "Do you play football?" he asked.

"Yep."

"Hey – give him a break!" Ali chided. "He's not even out of the hospital grounds yet."

"Are we going to McDonald's now?" Patrick tried impatiently.

Ali glanced at me apologetically. "We haven't had lunch yet – and I did promise him. D'you mind?"

"It's a great idea," I returned as Patrick whooped.

I felt like someone released from solitary confinement as sights and impressions hit me full on in the shopping centre. The traffic loud and grating, snippets of excited conversation, the smell of popcorn, perfume mingling with burgers and suddenly saturated with freshly ground coffee. It was like a different world, one that I hadn't been a part of for some weeks.

Just as I was beginning to experience the first blast of panic, Ali instinctively tightened her grip on my hand, guiding me through the bright swing doors of McDonald's. "Why don't you sit down and save us a table, while Patrick and I order?" she suggested.

"Thanks," I sank down gratefully, aware of how my legs were trembling. I suddenly felt weak and insubstantial.

"Anything you fancy in particular?" Ali questioned. "Or shall I just choose something?"

"Yeah – I'd be grateful if you did..."

Panicky feelings rose and fell as I watched the two of them become absorbed in the queue. The panic wasn't just because I had been out of normal circulation for at least three weeks; it was also because the Psyche had tapered my medication down and upped my mood stabilizers. Without those euphoric wings of Icarus to guide me close to the terrifyingly beautiful face of the sun, I was no longer Godlike, but instead mentally and emotionally impoverished by my growing sense of mortality. Hospital life had simultaneously sheltered and reduced me. Gratefully, I had slipped into becoming fully dependant on the clinical and medical staff who formed a protective membrane between the outside world and me.

As Patrick and Ali returned noisily with laden trays of goodies, I felt the panic in me subside. One of David Gray's soothing albums melted the fears into the background. When we were absolutely stuffed with deli sandwiches, French Fries and ice-cold coke, we talked about the future. Patrick was in hyper mode, chuntering on about football and his birthday which was tomorrow until, finally, Ali had sent him off with some pocket money so that we could have a bit of space to ourselves.

"Sorry about that!" Ali apologized. "He's been so looking forward to you coming to stay with us...and the fact that it's his birthday tomorrow has all but sent him over the edge."

I smiled. "Well – I hope I don't disappoint him," I grinned.

"I'm a boring old fart at the best of times."

Ali stroked my whiskery chin fondly. "I have to disagree with you there. For Patrick, you're the most exciting person he's come across since he grew out of Spiderman! You've broken your arm, your jaw and had black eyes that he would die for...You don't know how attractive that is to a ten year old boy!"

I shook my head, trying not to wince as I did so. "Obviously not...But I got beaten up, remember? There's hardly anything heroic about that!"

"Well, in Patrick's eyes, you fought that lowlife single handed...The fact you've got breaks and bruises to show for it makes you even more of a hotshot."

I shook my head. "Well – I'm flattered – but..."

Ali put a finger to my lips. "No buts – just accept."

I grinned, "Okay, I will."

"You look tired," Ali remarked, "and white...Pat should be back soon and we'll get you home."

Just as I was beginning to acknowledge my tiredness, how drained I felt, Patrick came bursting through the door with his latest purchases: sweets, comics and a sweatshirt with 'Manchester United' on.

"He doesn't get let out on the rampage very often," Ali explained. "And when he does, he makes up for it...He does a lot of work round the farm over weekends to earn pocket money and helps me, of course...So this is a one off."

By the time we arrived back at the farm, I felt like one of those lifeless jellyfish washed up on some foreign beach after a storm. I hadn't had so much activity or sensory information for weeks, it seemed. But my heart gave a double beat when the Range Rover swung up 'Buttercups Farm' driveway and I saw Moo sitting waiting for us at the door.

"I think she knew you were coming...She was restless all morning and wouldn't come in, just insisted on staying outside."

Moo mewed loudly and pushed against my hand as I bent

down to lift her up. Her purr was deep and throaty against my ear as I held her. "How have you been, my girl?" I asked gently, holding my emotions in abeyance. Moo didn't do emotional overspill.

I've got a companion, Moo purred. *I'd like you to meet him…*

Suddenly, the dark shadow that had been waiting concealed in the porch slinked into view. It was a large black tom with a white patch on its front like a dinner jacket. He was a substantial cat, about twice as big as Moo with an air of dignity about him. "I didn't realize you had a cat of your own," I said still holding Moo.

"That's Michael." Patrick explained. "He just arrived, last night. And he's staying to keep Moo company."

"Well – I don't know about that," Ali began. "He might belong to someone. He just arrived last night."

He belongs to me, Moo's distinctive voice announced to all those who could understand her. *He is my animal guardian and he comes from a very high place.*

She jumped down and padded purposefully over to the tom and they sniffed each other, rubbed noses as if they were lifelong friends.

"There, you see," Patrick chirruped. "They're buddies."

"But, if he belongs to someone they'll be missing him," Ali went on. "He doesn't look like a stray…Too well cared for…At least we have to ask around and see whether he's micro-chipped."

Vaguely, I remembered climbing the narrow staircase to my room, sinking down on the bed…And then I must have crashed out because I came to several hours later with the sensation of vibrating warmth around my neck which, I realized with delight, was Moo. Through the mullioned window I could hear the shrill cry of the swifts and the liquid warbling of the swallows overhead.

"Are you happy here?" I asked Moo.

Of course, she purred in that musical voice of hers.

"How did Michael come across you?" I asked.

Moo padded across my chest with slow deliberation. *I ordered him.*

"You ordered him?"

Moo licked her paw noisily and a drop of saliva fell onto my shirt. Because Moo had long hair, it took more saliva to wash, and in her enthusiasm, she would spray me with it. Not something I normally relished, but in our long shared absence, I almost welcomed it.

I knew that I needed someone to be with me on my travels in the days ahead. Michael is my soul mate. We've worked together, played together and fought together since the beginning of time on this earth – and before…Like me, Michael doesn't have to come here…It's voluntary…

"I see," I said knowledgably. "This is about evolution, Moo. Has he taken human form before?"

Moo licked her paw carefully before answering. *Yes…*

"And?"

…And he didn't much like it either so, like me, chose not to come back again – as a human. I couldn't help thinking that the way Moo articulated 'human' demoted it to a lower level of consciousness.

"So, you're both renegades?"

Well, Moo rubbed her paw behind one ear and then the other, simultaneously digging her claws into my chest, which seemed more purposeful than accidental. *We are…But no more than you are a renegade.*

"Owch!" I grimaced, trapped by both feline wit and claw. And then, dropping down into my psychotherapy role I voiced the proverbial question. "Why now, Moo? Why did you ask …or rather, order Michael to come?"

In a move of sheer procrastination, Moo arched her back, sunk her claws into my chest more delicately this time, and then settled again on me, meeting my gaze with her emerald one.

Because I'm going to need him now...I haven't been traveling to the Portal since you were...er, put out-of-action in hospital.

"Why?" I asked silently.

Moo looked at me loftily. *Because a cat's first priority is to guard their human kind. Humans, because of their chosen ignorance, aren't able to protect themselves psychically against intrusion...I had to protect you after those incarnated Nasym attacked you...They left you open and – anything could have got in.*

A chill ran through me and I had a fleeting image of that childhood feverish encounter with the fiery and iced forces that were fighting over my life.

Most animals can protect and shield humans from psychic attack, but domesticated cats have a very active role in this because they work so closely with humans...Psychic invasion from the Nasym are the most common form of possession and psychic sickness...Cats can erect a force field to prevent them from penetrating it.

"Why is Michael here, at this time?"

To protect the boy, Patrick...He's very vulnerable at his age...

"You mean my presence endangers him?"

Moo flicked her tail impatiently. *The combination of your presence and mine endangers him...But Michael is strong and as a male, he has the strength to protect a developing human male...*

"So, Michael is Patrick's cat!"

Yes.

"But he's your servant and does what you tell him," I said. "Because males on this planet have to obey 'She who rules'."

Moo, ignoring the comment, jumped onto the windowsill to gaze out onto her new surroundings. *I like it here...she* commented. *The energy is clear and we're quite well protected here from the outside world. Also the horses...She* added, hearing them whinnying. *They are good protectors. They are as strong in psychic protection as they are in muscle.* Closing her eyes, she lifted her head. *There is something deeper here...An ancient matrix of healing that goes back long before mankind...*

"Moo – do you talk to Patrick like this?"

No, of course not! she responded indignantly. *Children find it hard to hold onto such secrets...On one level, he'd want to keep it secret, but his excitement would betray him and that would endanger us, our relationship, because it wouldn't be long before the Nasym got to hear about it.*

"I'm relieved to hear that," I responded. "Have you talked any more to Ali?"

Moo's tail twitched. *You don't have to check up on me, I have a lot more awareness than most humans have about the work that I'm doing...*

"I don't dispute that."

Moo's tail twitched again. *No, I haven't spoken any more to her since that first time, which was very important and in dream form...But I've been using my image-work on her.* As Moo spoke, a tin of Somerfield tuna dropped into my mind.

"I see," I chuckled, wincing at the movement. "You certainly know how to look after yourself, Moo..."

Most cats do!

Chapter Sixteen

When in doubt, follow the Fur…
Gospel of Moo

I must have drifted off to sleep again because when I awoke, the room was swathed in darkness, aside from sudden and brief bursts of incandescence as the moon reappeared from behind fast scudding clouds. Checking my watch, I saw it was almost one in the morning. I had, somehow, managed to sleep most of the day and experienced a niggling sense of shame in this. Ali had gone to all this trouble to make me feel at home and I had crashed out without even thanking her. But tomorrow, or rather today, was Patrick's day and I was determined to make that as enjoyable for him as possible, since I was his only male father figure and something in me stirred with pride.

Just behind the curtain, on either side of the windowsill were Moo and Michael, tails twitching. They seemed unaware of me as they stared out of the window. On one level, I felt happy for Moo that she had a companion, yet on another, I felt I had lost a part of her that had belonged to me alone.

Suddenly aware of a genuine sense of hunger, I realized it had been lunch time since I had last eaten and groping around for a light switch near my locker, my hand brushed against a paper package. As the bedside light came on, I found Ali had left a small circular tray on the locker. Pulling it to me, I found a homemade sandwich, a rock cake and a thermos of fresh steaming coffee. I sank back gratefully; aware of a warmth flowing through me which came from knowing that someone genuinely cared for me enough to perform this small gesture of kindness…The bread was homemade and yeasty and I was grateful for having the crusts removed. I knew the hard-boiled eggs would be from the free-range chickens and the crumbly

Leicester style cheese would be made on the farm too.

I ate hungrily, but ever mindful of my bruised tongue and jaw if I moved it a certain way. I could see the cats sitting motionless on the windowsill; still seemingly unaware that I was watching them or even awake.

Later, when I padded across the landing in search of a toilet, my foot touched something half concealed under my bed. It was a brown paper bag with something pushed inside and a note attached. 'Hope you don't mind...This is your pressie to Pat...Love Ali.' The present was wrapped in Manchester United gift paper with Rooney and Nani heading balls across the paper. It was already addressed to Patrick from me and, very obviously, its spherical shape was something Patrick wouldn't be disappointed to receive. Ali had thought of everything and had even taken on two strange cats in the process.

After relieving myself in the bathroom, I hesitated on the landing as the floorboard creaked, listening to the sounds of the old farm cottage. Deeper still, lay the ambience of the generations that had preceded Ali. I paused outside the half open door of Ali's room to hear her snoring gently, and found that comforting. At the end of the corridor was Patrick's room and I remembered it, from the one time I'd stuck my head in briefly, as being a living altar to Manchester United. There were cups and medals on the dressers which Patrick had gleaned from his own matches or going to them. Scarves and streamers gathered dust against the wall.

Back in my room, Michael and Moo were still deeply engrossed in what appeared to be meditation, or whatever they were doing. Again I experienced a nostalgic sense of loss and yet I was glad Moo had this monster of a cat to protect her and keep her safe in a way I couldn't. Although I had been aware of the quiet gentleness the tomcat radiated, somehow this lay curled deep inside impenetrable steely depths. Funny how, like me, Ali had always been a dog person and yet now two cats owned us.

Ownership was definitely that way round, not the other.

As if sensing my thoughts, they both turned in unison to gaze at me, eyes luminous and ghostly in the full moon's incandescence. I held up my hands playfully. "Okay, mind readers," I tried, "I wasn't comparing, merely thinking."

They stared at me a while longer and then Michael turned back to the window, followed by Moo and they continued their shared meditation. For a while I lay there in the darkness, gazing in the direction of the window where the cats kept their vigil. Vaguely, in the background, I was aware of a high keening sound, eerily beautiful like the sound that the moon might make if it was audible, or a strange new planet as it waited to be discovered in the vast galaxies. Deeper still, a part of me even thought that it was the sound that a glacier or drifting iceberg might make.

I awoke to the sound of Patrick running bare-footed backwards and forwards along the landing, letting out a whoop every now and then. This was followed by a 'shush' from Ali. "It's early still, Pat," she explained. "Pete needs his rest."

I smiled to myself as this was met by an exclamation of protest. "It's eight o'clock Saturday morning, Mum...How much sleep does he need?"

"Well, another hour...Why don't you go and play outside?"

Another groan of protest. "Play with what? I want my presents!"

My grin widened as I called out. "Hey, Patrick, why don't you come in here, Birthday Boy, and see what I've got for you!"

"He's awake!" Patrick whooped before he dashed into my room, grinning at me as his excited gaze scanned the room, settling on the present. "Is that mine?"

"You bet." I tossed it towards him with my good arm. "Here catch!"

He caught it eagerly. "Aw, wicked! I know what this is gonna be!"

Ali tapped on the door, came in and sighed exasperatedly.

"There's no stopping him! He's been like an unleashed dynamo since five o'clock this morning. I'm sorry."

"Don't be," I countered. "I'm fine about it…. Really!"

We both stared at Patrick. His cheeks were flushed as the red Manchester United ball appeared. "Oh cool," he said, turning it over. "It's got all their signatures on it, Rooney, Nani, Hargreaves…"

"What do you say?" Ali prompted.

"Thanks Pete," he chirped, cheeks flushed as he flung his arms around my waist. "That's just what I wanted." He bounced it on the floor, off his knee and then dribbled it along the hallway. "Can I play with it before breakfast?" he asked Ali.

"Go on then," Ali said. "But I think you might want something to go with that ball." Look in the kitchen. Down by the washer…" Her voice trailed off as Patrick took the stairs two at a time and ran into the kitchen. "Were you ever like that?" she asked.

"Manic? Yes. Frequently," I laughed. "But football crazy, I wasn't…I was just into running, long distance, short distance, cross country – relay."

She smiled, giving me one of those famous bear hugs, hugely modified to suit my broken and bruised body. "I'm so glad you're here," she said. "It's going to be great to have you around too…Pat drives Joey up the wall with all his questions…He has a few friends of his own but not close ones he can bring home, apart from George…She's a girl, a real tomboy. She'll be coming round to celebrate his birthday with him tonight. It'll be good to have someone more his age around him. I worry about him being an only child and whether he'll be too grown up before his time."

"I don't think there's much sign of that at the moment," I tried.

There was a whoop of joy from downstairs in the kitchen.

"Sounds like he's found what you wanted him to find…"

"Hey, come down here you two…It's a coaching net, a real

football net. Help me put it up, Pete!"

Dutifully, I held one end of the net as Patrick assembled it and decided to put it on the other side of a disused barn, away from the bantams and cock.

"Thanks Mum," he said, hugging her, his cheeks flushed with excitement. "It's great...Oh, this is going to be such a great day. Pete, will you teach me to score some goals after I've had a warm up?"

"Okay," I agreed, thinking to myself that he probably had more to teach me, than I ever could. "Eggs, hash browns and mushrooms in about half an hour," Ali called out to him.

"'kay Mum," Pat acknowledged, dribbling the ball.

"I take it you slept well," Ali smiled. "I poked my head in several times but you were sound."

"I slept like a baby. It was wonderful not to have bells ringing, machines bleeping and someone testing my obs every couple of hours. I'm afraid I've been so conked out that I haven't had the chance to thank you."

"What for?" Ali returned, slicing the potatoes and arranging them in a large pan where slices of beefsteak tomatoes were gently simmering. "You've been so good for Pat...Or rather your cat has been. You know, since she came to live here a week ago, Pat hasn't had any nightmares or wet the bed...He had a pantheon of disturbing dreams about some bogeyman...He'd call out and I thought he was going to suffocate; he'd been breathing so raggedly...I even took him to the Doc. Fat lot of good that was...Just said it would pass and it was the usual angst some boys of his age go through from a broken home."

"Broken home! Did he say that? Tactless bugger!"

"But..." Ali brushed away an angry tear. "He's right...Pat's always missed having a Dad or even an older brother and sister."

"Hey, Ali, don't do this to yourself! You know this is a pattern of yours, self-recrimination. He's a great kid and you were saying Moo had helped him."

"Yes, she has..." She broke the eggs into the pan and basted them, then stirred the mushrooms into a buttery garlic sauce. "He just said that having Moo made him feel safe."Her voice broke off. "How can a cat make him feel safe when I can't do that for him? His own mother!"

"I felt safe with Fly, my dog...But Moo makes me feel safe too, if that's any consolation, and I'm not a young boy haunted by the bogeyman."

"And she makes me feel safe too," Ali admitted.

"Maybe Michael makes Moo feel safe too!"

We both laughed.

"Who makes you feel safe?" Patrick asked breathlessly, sinking down in the chair.

"Moo," we both chorused.

"And Michael makes me feel safer still," Patrick said. "He's cool, and once, he spoke to me!"

"He did?" Ali said, egg poised on the spatula in mid air. "What did he say?"

"I can't tell you that, Mum," Patrick responded soberly. Watch out, you're going to drop that egg..."

The egg slid off the spoon and I just managed to catch it on Patrick's plate, but not before it splattered sunny side down, bright orange yolk running everywhere.

"Ugh Mum, I'm not having that!"

"I'll have it," I said and exchanged plates. "A broken egg is good luck!"

"Is it?" Ali and Patrick chorused.

"Why not?" I dunked my bread in it.

I ate hungrily as though I had run a marathon rather than slept through a marathon. Moo sauntered in, mewed for a saucer of fresh warm milk, rubbed against me, against all of us in turn and then went out the door into the sunlight where the swallows were warbling over the barn outside. I thought, any moment I would wake up in hospital to find that I was dreaming.

As if the cooked breakfast wasn't enough, Ali tempted me with a hunk of bread and passed me a jar of honey. "Made locally," she grinned. "Very locally!"

By the bees of Buttercup Farm," Patrick piped."I can take you to see them after."

"Bees! You keep bees?"

Ali mopped her bread round the plate, gathering up the last remnant of mushroom juice. "Yep…I only have three hives at the moment but they keep us in honey all year." She smiled. "Actually, they were here long before I came. I just inherited them.

I ladled the spoon onto my bread and smacked my lips. "Gorgeous. Is there anything you don't do, Ali Mcalpine?"

"Play football!" Pat put in quickly. "She can't even kick a ball…" He inspected my plaster. "Do you mind if I write on it?"

"Feel free," I invited. "Everyone else has…At least, every patient and member of staff on the ward."

Patrick studied the multi-colored autographing meticulously. "You've got the ward manager here, staff nurses and are these other names patients?"

"Some of them!"

He poured over it. "Anybody famous?"

"Not that I know of."

He peered at some writing by the elbow in red. "There's one here…"

I strained to see. "I hadn't noticed that. What does it say?"

"It says 'follow the fun, love from Terry, the yellow canary.'"

Involuntarily, I snatched my arm away and was aware of the roar of blood in my ears, my heart pounding…

"No," Ali corrected, gently moving my arm back, squinting at the red scrawl on my elbow through bifocals. "It says … 'Follow the fur'." She smiled. "Whoever wrote it must have known you kept a cat!"

"Why did he call himself the yellow canary?" Patrick quizzed.

"Because he was yellow…" I began slowly, my voice strangely disembodied as if I was standing outside myself looking in. "The medical term is 'jaundiced', it means yellow."

"Oh? Why do people get yellow?"

"It's when the liver isn't functioning properly," Ali explained patiently. "When people have yellow skin and the whites of their eyes are yellow, it means the blood contains a lot of a waste substance called 'bilirubin' which should have been got rid of through the liver, bile or kidneys…It can be caused by a virus or through using badly infected needles, through drug taking or through drinking a lot of alcohol…"

"I'm impressed," I said. "How do you know all this?"

"Long story really," Ali toyed with her plate. "Before I took all this psychotherapy and coaching lark on board, I trained to be a doctor."

"Wow, Mum!" Pat sighed. "I didn't know that…So you're a Doc…Cool!"

"Let me finish," Ali countered firmly. "Don't keep inter-rupting…I left during the last six months. I didn't qualify."

"Why Mum?"

Ali sighed. "As I said, it's a long story and I'll probably tell you one day…Ask me in a few years, Pat…But we're not talking about me…We're talking about this man with jaundice."

"Yes, Terry, the yellow canary. Why did he go yellow, Pete? Was it an infection?"

"I don't know." I said this, even though I knew Terry had been an alcoholic. I don't know why I knew he was an alcoholic, but I did. The same way I knew that when he had signed my arm, he had already been pronounced clinically dead. The kitchen, always so comforting and cool with the steady ticking of the Grandmother Clock suddenly felt cramped and airless. I had to get outside.

Distantly, I heard Patrick call after me to play football with him, and then Ali's surprisingly firm voice saying, "he needs his space right now…Let him be…He'll play later."

I found myself over by the horses, the Shire horse, Viktor, who moved easily and powerfully towards me to nuzzle my hand to see whether it contained any goodies. And then when it didn't, he gave a snort and swung his head to drive the ever-present flies away. Stacey, Patrick's pony, came over and left her head within reach so that I could scratch between her ears. As I did this, I noticed the plaster on my arm was beginning to itch like hell, and I stared at the red ink at the elbow. 'Follow the fur.' It wasn't that I hadn't any memory of his ever writing that on my arm, it was those compelling words. As if in some way he knew about Moo and her Philosophy of Fur. It was unsettling and had me even wondering whether, in some wildly unhinged moment, I had written it myself, except I knew I hadn't. It wasn't my writing. But, I knew that there was a part of me, the part that was struggling to hang onto frayed threads of sanity, which wanted to believe I had, somehow, written it myself.

I was grateful for my time alone. I had almost stopped breathing after finding Terry's signature on my plaster. And it was such a gorgeous day. Distantly, I was aware of the screaming of the swifts overhead as they fell like arrows behind the hedge and into the stream, rising moments later to soar into the cloudless sky again. High in the barn, the swallows warbled and trilled in liquid cadences as they reclaimed their nests that had survived the long winter. Reclaimed the barn, just as their parents had done along with the generations before them. In this miraculous day where I was surrounded by beauty and goodwill, a terrible fear lurked like the snake in the Garden of Eden. A snake that presaged a terrible fall if I allowed myself to forget or, like the ill fated Icarus, fly too high.

Just in front of the orchard, I stopped short of three latticed white boxes and it took me a few seconds to comprehend what they were. They stood there like Sylvia Plath's 'coffins', waiting for me to discover them. But then I saw Moo lying directly beneath one of them and my heart softened. Her head was held up so that her small black nose pointed to the sky. Her ears were slightly back and her eyes were closed. She looked euphoric, just as I remembered she had those months ago when I had seen her sitting under my buddleia in an ecstatic trance. Remembering how Moo loved bees, I sank down in the long grass and closed my eyes too, happy to be with her, listening to her beloved bees with their furry golden vests.

I breathed deeply of the morning air, redolent with the fragrance of grass, blossom, gorse and buddleia, and I was filled with an unassailable sense of freedom which swept me right back to childhood. Back to the time when summers seemed to stretch on and on into an idyllic eternity. Summers when I would be out riding on my bike before the majority of the world kick-started their daily routine. I would pedal as fast as I could through the country lanes with the trees on either side latticing their branches in a green archway. I could remember how the breeze would comb through the cherry and apple blossom so that it cascaded along the winding roads in an endless trail of confetti. Early morning bumble bees, still dozy with sleep, bounced past me as they careered clumsily through the webbed branches in their search for nectar. With only the milkman out on his rounds, I felt in control of my world, omnipotent and supremely free. Yet, even then, a shadow presaged the idyllic ambience around me. As a young boy who experienced freedom and confidence within the parameters of my world, I knew that this wouldn't last forever. That's why I had to make the most of it; milk every moment of its freedom before everything changed from sunlight to shadow. And as if to drive this awareness from my mind, I would resume my furious pedaling. Pedal until everything around me was a blur and the pedals whizzed round and round without me.

I came to, taking in my surroundings, the buzz of bees collecting precious pollen; the shrill of swifts as they sliced the air, the butterflies on the buddleia and Moo…. Moo under the beehive, head lifted, lost in that ecstatic trance that I was becoming more and more to envy. A trance where she was somewhere ensconced in folds of fur or dowsing the *Mooisphere* with those long silken whiskers of hers.

I was startled out of my reverie by a low deep 'meow' at my side and looked down to see Michael at my feet. I reached down to stroke his head, noticing the thicker coarser texture of his fur and the muscular more substantial build of his body. "Well, old boy," I whispered. "We're all having a little meditation here and you're welcome to join us."

Michael gave a little mew and jumped up on the stone bench beside me. I heard his throaty purr reach an even keel as we looked to where Moo was still seated in her seemingly ecstatic trance under one of the hives. Her presence did not bother the bees any more than they bothered her.

"Well, mate," I whispered. "Welcome to morning meditation!"

Michael looked up at me, making an acknowledging sound at the back of his throat, which was a cross between a purr and a mew.

"You're certainly much appreciated round here…Patrick's stopped having nightmares and I'm happy for Moo…" My voice trailed off as I was aware again of that sense of sadness as though I had lost Moo on some level or other.

You will never lose Moo, came the deep voice beside me.

My heart thudded loudly as I turned to stare into the tom's amber eyes. "You can speak too!" Then, realizing how arrogant I sounded, added clumsily, "or rather…you choose to communicate with me."

You will never lose Moo, Michael repeated. *You saved her life once…Long ago.*

As if by reply, an image swam into my mind of a seal being pursued by a fishing boat. Then men were cheering and shouting. Dressed in reindeer skin they called out in a language although foreign, I seemed to understand.

"Faster...We've almost got her...She's tiring..."

The seal's nostrils were flaring, straining for air and I could see that she was fighting for her life. But then as our eyes met, I saw further, deeper, as if I could see into her soul. She was pregnant and her pup was due, just a day away, even sooner with this stress. As our eyes met, it was as if I could see into her soul. Distantly, I heard myself reply to them in their language. "It's okay...I'm nearer...I'll get her."

The men hesitated only briefly, knowing and trusting me with their unspoken words. As they slowed down, I turned my boat as if to go after the seal that was almost level with me. I reached for the net to throw it, knowing that I could effortlessly draw her in. She would not fight much because she was gripped by a deep exhaustion. And then, skillfully, I wedged my foot in the netting and feigned being rendered helpless and, at the last moment, as the seal drew level with the boat, I wobbled over the edge, taking the boat with me so that it capsized. I knew I was taking a risk, not just with my fellow hunters, but even more dangerously within the icy water itself. A man, however strong, could not last more than minutes in those subzero temperatures, even with the seal oil most hunters rubbed into their skin before each hunting trip as insulation. As the waters closed over my head and I allowed myself to sink into the icy depths, I wondered at the stupidity of what I had just done. And yet it was as if the soul of the seal had reached into mine and pleaded with me to save her life. Yet this act of sabotage was a deeply shameful act; for I had a wife and child to care for and the meat of the seal would feed all our families for several days. Unborn seal pup was prize meat too. Paralyzed by this deepening sense of shame, I allowed myself to sink even further until my natural survival instincts electrified me into action, even as my lungs were burning. I kicked powerfully upwards to find several strong hands reaching for me, grasping my shoulders strongly and hauling me into the bottom of the boat. Silently, exhaustedly, we took it in turns to row back to the shore. The silence between us was one of exhaustion rather than accusation...

Memories unfolded and I gazed in pride at my eight-year-old son dressed in sealskin boots and parka. In his hand he had a mock harpoon, emulating a big hunt as young boys do as they dream of their initiation into manhood, into tribal ways. Around his neck he wore a single walrus tooth. This was his totem animal and I could see the bravery and strength already evident in his stance and behavior. My wife with her dark coal colored hair held out her arms, welcoming me back to the fire, showing relief instead of disappointment at my failed hunting expedition. Looking into her green eyes and taking in her wide welcoming smile, there was a sense of deep recognition inside me, but it was a recognition I couldn't place because it lay somewhere beyond the boundaries of time.

Just before I left the deep reverie I was aware of another day dawning and within its wake, there were excited joyful voices. I smelled the sea, heard the waves and came to as the woman jerked me awake. "All is not lost," she said, in that strange guttural language I seemed to understand so well. "The Gods have brought us a gift," she began breathlessly. "Come and see!"

Painfully, I rose up, the air hurting my strained lungs as I breathed and saw two shapes on the shore surrounded by tribal people I recognized as kith and kin. And there was my boy, his feet stamping out the hunter's dance.

"Porpoises!" My wife exclaimed. "Two of them, ran ashore this morning...Not long dead and the Shaman has inspected them. They are good...Good meat...Enough for us all for half a moon at least."

I grinned from ear to ear and thought. "Yes, the Gods have been kind..."

Slowly, I came back to my present surroundings. The feel of the wind stirring the trees; the scent of apple blossom and coconut gorse and the steady, almost hypnotic, buzz of the bees. I looked at Michael and thought, "That seal I saved was Moo, wasn't it?"

That's why you can't lose each other, Michael responded. *You are bound by ancient laws that wield the fabric of life and death.*

Deep relief filled me along with a sense that as whacky as this all sounded to the logical mind, a deep irrefutable truth underlay all of this otherworldly experience that I was enmeshed in. At the very best, it created a solid and credible template to build my future on. At the very worst, I could torture myself with this reality, believing that I was 'losing it' and plunging deep into a terrifying psychotic abyss where there was little sense of return. But I checked myself. I had a strong sense of self, an observing self, where I could pan out from my emotions and feelings rather than collapsing into the experience. I was stronger now. Only weeks ago, before I had landed myself in hospital, I had been inwardly fragile. Inside, I was aware of a growing strength and sense of rightness in everything. Within this matrix of wellbeing was an emerging sense of aligning myself to the three most important qualities of life beyond the survival instinct. These were meaning, purpose and values. The meaning came from my present circumstances, being at the farm with Moo, Ali and Patrick and, although I knew it couldn't last forever, everything changed, it was right for now. Purpose was in discovering what was waiting for me in this experience and value would come from that. More than anything, there was a deep sense of Self, of spirit, of a power greater than myself in this. This power came from a deeply spiritual experience rather than a religious one. "Is Moo all right?" I asked Michael. "I mean, is she well?"

We both looked at Moo who still seemed lost in her blissful state with the bees.

She's fine, Michael returned. *She's refueling – gathering energy for the times ahead.*

"Times ahead?"

Michael, as if wanting to bring the topic to a close, jumped neatly down and padded over to where Moo was and lay a little distance away from her in the long grass.

I was just wandering what shape these 'times ahead' would take when Patrick charged over to me out of nowhere. "Oh, there you are!" he announced with breathless impatience. "I've been looking for you everywhere." He tugged my arm. "Come on, watch me score some goals."

Reluctantly, I left my resting place and followed him back to the cottage and across to where we had set out the coaching net. He then entertained me with ten or eleven goals before passing the ball to me with 'beat that' bravado. "Now, you have a go!"

"Okay," I said, dribbling the ball, "but I'm not at my best."

"Go on," said Patrick. "Just put one in."

My first bounded off the goal post, but the second and third slammed into the net and Patrick whooped with joy. "And another...And another..."

"Here's someone to see you," Ali announced as a girl with curly golden hair, dressed in shorts, trainers and Adidas shirt, dashed out to tackle the ball off Patrick.

"I think Patrick might have met his match there with Georgie," another taller woman with the same golden hair laughed. "She's been practicing all morning, and almost broke the next door neighbor's window in the process...And he wasn't in the least bit impressed." She moved forward to shake my hand and I noticed that she was younger than Ali. "I'm Karen."

"Pleased to meet you," I returned.

"Ali told me about that unfortunate event with those thugs and tells me that you'll be convalescing here for a while." Her handshake was warm and friendly as was her voice. "I hope you get better soon...Hey...Georgie," she called. "Come and say 'hello' to Pete."

Dutifully, Georgie broke away from her game and shook my hand. "Good to meet you," she said. "Patrick's told me all about you!"

"Has he?"

Georgie smiled. "Oh, only good things," she flushed. "Like how brave you are...He *likes* you!"

Ali ushered us through the kitchen and into the garden with its herb garden rockery and its rows of early spring onions, potatoes and peas showing through. Outside she had arranged wicker chairs around a shaded wicker table. Tall glasses of homemade iced lemonade were arranged on a tray next to plates of salted peanuts, cashews, pecans, crisps and cracker snacks. On an adjoining table were plates of sandwiches, sausages, cheese and onion rolls, slices of quiche, an assortment of savory and sweet tarts and trifle covered with layers of cream.

"Aw cool, Mum!" Patrick expressed with pleasure. "Thanks."

"I'm afraid we'll all have to put up with Manchester United napkins," Ali said handing them out. "I forgot to buy any others."

Again, I found all the fresh air combined with all the homemade cooking made me absolutely famished and I ate like I had been on a long expedition and not eaten for days. While we adults discussed growing vegetables, keeping hens and rearing goats, Georgie and Patrick slipped effortlessly in and out of focus with plates of sandwiches, lemonade and crisps. Then there was the chocolate and fudge birthday cake, which Karen took the credit for baking. While Pat blew out the candles to our applause, I looked on, experiencing a warmth and sense of belonging that I hadn't experienced in years. While the children continued playing football, scoring goals, dribbling across the yard, Ali and Karen talked about Nick, her husband, being away in Edinburgh on business where he had a rapidly growing recording company. I watched the swallows flying to and from the barn with nesting material to repair the winter's damage.

Much later, after Karen had left with a reluctant Georgie to go home, I lingered out in the garden. Even though the air had cooled now that the sun was sinking, I breathed deeply of the evening air, as if I was never going to experience this again. Hospital memories were still too close to render this thought an impossibility.

"Hey," Ali's voiced pulled me back. "Do you fancy a celebratory glass of wine after a very long and successful day?"

"I'd rather have a hug," I said, holding my good arm out in invitation.

As I felt the soft warmth of Ali against my chest, the familiar scent of rose and patchouli seemed to draw me in further. And before I could stop myself, I was kissing her with a sudden hungry passion that had my heart racing and there was an unmistakable stirring in my loins. But Ali, rather than withdrawing, seemed to press herself into me so that I could feel her hard nipples against me and involuntarily my hand slipped down to tease them through her blouse and one of us moaned.

Chapter Seventeen

These openings to the Portal are still accessible today and people seek out the deep peace of these sanctuaries often without really knowing why. Those who do understand why, keep quiet about it.
Gospel of Moo

I am ashamed to say that after that sudden burst of passion, our relationship didn't progress in the way it might have done if responsibilities and fears hadn't been paramount. The feelings were still there though, burning and crackling in the background and often in the foreground.

We might have graduated to degree level in psychotherapy but when it came to our own personal relationship, we became autistic. After that kiss, the physical part of our relationship was left hanging. Anyone from a non-counseling background would have mirrored back our denial of what was happening, along with the fear that if we allowed ourselves to be swept away by our feelings, we could lose what we had. To go further, which meant opening up to possible loss, could reopen those old historical wounds and create fresh painful history between us. Not only that, but a ten-year-old child was involved. The fact that we were behaving like dysfunctional teenagers rather than consensual adults, said a lot about our historical wounds. I don't know whether Ali felt the same as I did; on fire with longing, yet tortured by a sense of pending loss if we gave further fuel to that fire.

I could understand my own reasons for reticence; the fear of shattering what promised to be an idyllic respite from more pressing issues; of how I could earn money to pay my bills. Deeper still, were questions around when, or even, whether I should return to my flat with Moo...But what was there to return to? With my manic episode, I'd had to cancel taking on any new clients indefinitely and others had trailed off discouraged by the lack of continuity in sessions and probably my counseling persona. And then there was the attack that had precipitated this change in circumstance, my time in hospital to 'landing on my feet' here. Did I want to return to revisit the incident that had violently punched a hole through the fabric of my life in the flat? Right now, I needed to rest and simultaneously begin to rebuild a plan of action. But, not now! Definitely, not now!

But still, every time I saw Ali, thought of her, the air buzzed and crackled between us like barbecued bacon.

Things were happening with Moo.

Her sense of peace and quiet joy was beginning to fracture into discomfort. As much as she spent most of the day seated by the beehives, her chin lifted in that rapturous pose, at night she was agitated, restless. My concern would be ameliorated by Moo's presence back in my bedroom, sitting on my chest as she often did in the old days. Facing me, eyes thin green slits, she would purr as she communicated to me in that voice I had grown to love and welcome so much. During these nocturnal sessions I would learn about the witches that had been persecuted throughout Europe in the seventeenth century. This merciless persecution had taken place over three centuries, culminating in their mass execution throughout the seventeenth century. Before that, Moo explained, the communications between the more ethereal worlds were common to many. The witches were the keepers of the Portal and they sent their cats backwards and forwards to bring medicine and healing to those in need. The Portal, in those days, had many entrances into the physical world. Then, it was a life force of pure light, which ran in tributaries throughout the landscape. The water, away from the smog of the cities, was sparkling and alive. The witches with their cats or familiars understood the needs of their community and could alleviate many of the psychic illnesses that afflicted its members. But then the church wanted more power over the masses and sought to exercise control over these witches or Keepers of the Portal and their familiars, until the landscape far and wide ran with blood and the earth groaned with the pain of tortured bodies that it had so lovingly created. In the greed for power and control of behavior and thought that deviated from the body of the Church, the understanding of spirituality became lost. In its place, the implacable institution of religion was erected and ruled. Spirituality was akin to the air that people breathed; their heavenly inspiration. Religion was the edifice that imprisoned the heart and soul. Without spirituality there was no fragrance to attract the bees to the pollen. Man's impoverished self fell into unconsciousness while the church fought over ownership of the soul; that part which could never be possessed.

"What happened then Moo – to the Portal?"

The tributaries that were linked to the Portal went underground, Moo continued. *They were no longer needed and those who did experience the pain of their absence, were too afraid to access them for fear of what the Papal authorities would do.*

"What about the cats? The witches' familiars?"

Moo had long stopped purring. *They kept a low profile. Withdrew from the towns and cities and moved to places where the Portal was still accessible.*

"Where were these places that had access?"

The forests and woods, Moo replied. *It was in these strong silent places that animals felt secure and less hunted by man. It was also where people began to slowly pilgrimage. These openings to the Portal are still accessible today and people seek out the deep peace of these sanctuaries often without really knowing why. Those who do understand why, keep quiet about it. The older a stand of trees was, the deeper the contact with the Portal...That's why cats love climbing trees...Even if many have forgotten about their origins; they still feel this connection with the trees and are inspired by them. It's as if they know that trees are rooted deep in their history...Some people who love trees are aware of this too...*

"But then people began to chop down the woods and forests."

Yes...And it wasn't just for wood and timber, it was because of a deep fear of the forests. To anyone who had exiled all awareness of the Portal from their consciousness, the woods appeared dark and oppressive. Above all, they could not control nature. It could grow while their backs were turned and within the woodland were forces and energies that humans could no longer understand. These, in animal lore, were known as the breathing corridors to the other worlds.

Moo paused to lick her paw.

All these breathing corridors have been in danger of being cut down, but for one thing...

"We need them to breathe. By cutting them down we add to the carbon dioxide," I grimaced. "Really there isn't much hope for us," I added bleakly.

Moo concentrated on biting her claws, nibbling out the granules of dirt that lodged inside. *But that's why we need people like you.*

I waited for Moo to go on and offer an explanation, but her silence was an invitation to probe further.

"Okay – what can I do Moo?"

You can help keep the Portals clear. Help maintain them.

"How?"

But I already knew. It had something to do with working with the Nasym, the souls that were pouring through the main Portal where animals sought human form in order to escape the carnage and endless slaughter of the animals. These were animal souls that were so injured that they would do anything to escape animal bondage.

"I don't think I could do that, Moo,"

Of course you can't! Moo returned sharply, pulling off a slice of claw in irritation so that we both winced. *You have to be trained. You can't just go in there cold.*

I looked at her blankly.

I am going to introduce you to the Portal, or at least one of its openings.

I wanted to ask if I had a choice. But deep down I knew I hadn't. Moo, for some reason, had chosen me and with that came all the karmic baggage, as the Buddhists believed. Deep down, for some reason, I believed this too.

Over the next few days, Moo told me about the entrances to the Portal; that they spanned the world. *They're not just in the forests,* she explained. *Forests and woods are merely corridors to the Portal.* Her green eyes held mine, and she began to purr softly. *Where do you think the entrances to the Portal might lie?* she probed. *You have to think from that deep place inside you…"*

I thought and relaxed enough to enter what I had come to know as the *Mooisphere.*

I seemed to enter a dimension of warm downy fur and whiskers. It's as if I could feel the visceral effect of the whiskers or, rather, stubble on my face, dowsing, dowsing the *Mooisphere.* Against my will, I was drawn to places where there had been recent calamities; the Tsunami in the Indian Ocean…I could see the people running, the crash of water, the sound was deafening. Trees being ripped like toothpicks from the ground, the terrifying maelstrom and then the silence afterwards…Then I saw the Burmese Cyclone, tearing houses, trees, everything from the earth. The whole landscape seemed to become wrenched up out of matter and shaken violently, then dropped …And then the silence and underneath the tectonic plates in the Indian Ocean and Burma buckling. But underneath, deeper, there was light…Blinding light. And then my attention was drawn to the latest earthquake in China, the ground and the roads buckling buildings, falling like a pack of cards. People crying out, running. Faces ashen with dust or smattered with blood. Then Haiti…People buried alive, typhoid, rape, looting…But, underneath all of this…

The light…

It was brilliant, warm, blinding, and within this light I saw hundreds and thousands of souls rising up from the carnage like motes of dust in the sunlight. At first their features were distinct, then they became smaller, surrendering their form to become golden dust, cascading into...And here, I had to shield my eyes, a vast chasm of light. All the noise dispersed; there was only a deep silence. Not an empty silence, but one that was pregnant. No, overflowing - with such healing. No more, much more, love. Great Love...

The power was great, ancient and seemed to make my hair bristle, not just on my head, but on my arms and legs, the backs of my hands.

These are the places that are directly connected to the Portal. Where the earth has opened and there has been loss of lives and homes. This is where the light breaks through like ocean waves upon a turbulent beach.

"Why do these terrible things happen though, Moo?" I asked. "Is it a form of punishment?"

Moo gave a low growl. *You humans always think in terms of punishment and retribution, loss and success, but you can't measure the working out of these things in that way. It's too mechanistic...These things happen because it's the way of the earth, the Mooisphere, the Great Purr...*

"You're not making any sense, Moo..."

Light enters the earth through catastrophe and loss and pours through in the broken places, so that healing can take place there. You see, nothing is ever lost on the level where it matters. Everything, all life, returns to the Great Purr and is reborn with its own individual life journey ahead of it within the Collective. Moo paused to avidly scratch her back, sending tufts of fur flying.

"But when people lose their lives, Moo, their loved ones, their homes everything they own, it's terrible..."

I know...It's the same with animals, in the finite sense, but you don't lose them forever. Souls live on. They re-incarnate...It's always painful for those left behind because they have to pick up the pieces. Start again. Draw on resources within themselves that may never have come into operation before. Deeply spiritual resources that may have atrophied if the disaster hadn't happened.

"What good can come of world catastrophe?"

Moo sighed. *Again you're thinking like humans do. In black and white, good and bad, beautiful and ugly...I can't communicate through the medium of these terms...*

"What is the reason and purpose behind them?" I tried.

Moo sighed. *'Reason' I don't understand because it's man-made. But, purpose I can understand,* she began to purr. *Purpose is not time bound or circumstance bound. Purpose unites and elevates the working out of situations. Purpose unites and inspires individual work to the common good of all. Purpose is a foundation stone that nothing can shatter. Catastrophes, after the aftermath, connect individuals to collective purposes and goals. With you humans, everything is linear which has enormous limitations. You build more and more. You want more and more. You have more and more. You stockpile on every level because...*

"Because?" I urged, and then as Moo started scratching again, I withdrew involuntarily. "Moo, you've got fleas!"

No, I haven't! Came the quick retort.

"Yes, you have... Owch! One just bit me!" I yelped.

After that, as I pinned the hard shelled flea down to the table, our discussion ended abruptly with Moo trotting off, ears back, to the kitchen and me cursing under my breath as I set to work bundling the duvet cover, sheets, pillow cases and anything else I could find, in the washing machine. Later, while I was waiting for the washing to run its cycle with a mug of strong coffee, I fumigated my bedroom with flea repellent.

"I wouldn't blame Moo for the fleas," Ali began, joining me in a black coffee. "The fleas have been here long before Moo or Michael arrived..." She cupped the mug in her hands and peeped at me rather sheepishly over the rim with those liquid caramel eyes of hers. "They've always been around on the farm. They come in from the stables every year. I've tried borax and salt which seem to help for a while," she shrugged, "I don't notice them any more…Besides, I think they've given up biting me. Hey, do you fancy a ride this morning?"

A welcome distraction. "Horse riding?" My heart leapt. "That's the best invitation I've had in ages. I'd love to, Ali…"

"Has it been long since you last rode?"

"About six months."

"How's your arm, by the way?"

I flexed it. "Almost as good as new. Just very stiff."

"Well, that's settled then." She drained her mug and shook her hair off her face. "I'll ride Pegasus and you can take the gelding for now. He's got a good temperament…Doesn't get so easily fazed, and they're used to your smell around the place now."

"There's something I have to do first," I said, already standing up to leave. "I'll only be about twenty minutes."

Ali shrugged. "No rush…I thought we could have breakfast first, or at least some toast…I'm starved."

I knew where I would find Moo, in her usual place under the beehives and I hurried over there for the sole reason of apologizing for my hasty apportioning blame on her for the fleas. But I drew up sharply when I saw the white beehives with no Moo sitting underneath. I tried calling for her, but could get no response and then I turned on my feet and headed in the direction of the barn. The swallows had now had their young and they were scything backwards and forwards, beaks laden with grubs and insects. Just momentarily, I experienced a sense of unease as if a part of me had reached out to search for her and just hit a blank. No! A wall!

"Moo?" I called. "I'm really sorry about the fleas…I now know where they came from…Moo?"

I sank down on the bench dejectedly, knowing that I wouldn't be able to enjoy my ride with Ali unless I had made amends with Moo. Poor Moo. I had injured her dignity at a time when she was imparting some of her wisdom, which could help me, if not the human race. But there was no sign of Moo. After I sought out all her favorite places, I returned to the beehives dejectedly. Moo had simply vanished and I couldn't blame her for sulking...As I sat there, all the old fears around Moo came flooding back. Supposing she had vanished for good and had decided not to come back from wherever she'd gone? I couldn't imagine a life without Moo. As crazy as it seemed, she was my best friend and I felt incomplete without her....

I came to as Michael jumped up on the bench beside me and pushed his large head into my hand. *What is it, Old Boy?* he asked.

"I've lost Moo... Do you know where she is?"

Michael's amber eyes looked into mine. *She's gone far away,* he spoke into my mind. *But it isn't because of anything you said or didn't say...She's been preparing to go for quite some time.*

"Go?" Sandpaper was wedged in the back of my throat as I croaked. "Go where?"

Where do you think Moo would go?" Michael asked. *She tells me you've been her student for all her life...You must have learned something by now?*

Michael was right. I was acting like a parent who had just lost their child when, in actual fact, as far as Moo was concerned, she was the adult and I was the recalcitrant student. I closed my eyes and calmed myself as Moo had told me to do, and then reached inside myself to find that part which would connect with the *Mooisphere.* All I could hear was the humming of bees. I breathed more slowly, sank deeper and just for a split second felt a connection with warm fur...Moo...Then it was gone. Patrick's voice called me back. "Mum's said toast is ready..."

"Okay," I flung back. "Just coming..."

I sat for a while longer, breathing slowly but still looking for Moo.

She'll be back, Michael assured me. *You just go and enjoy your day.*

Chapter Eighteen

The days passed at the farm, riding with Ali and Patrick as well as working on the land, I began to experience a new strength in my limbs and vitality in my body. And with it all emerged a dawning surety that my relationship with Ali was a secure friendship that I could depend on. We were comfortable around each other and, to be honest, I would rather have it this way than a passionate sexual roller coaster where emotions carried me into a fire I had no control over. Not that the feelings weren't there for me at least. But they were held in abeyance. I was grateful for the hard physical work each day with the help of Joey, the stable hand, who could turn his skill to tackle most things. While I milked the cow, managed the tractor, learned to rotavate the soil; creating areas for the sweet corn, potatoes, runners and broad beans, Patrick milked the goats, looked after the hens, feeding them grain, cleaning out their area and adding it to the growing compost. When I wasn't working outside on the farm, I was giving Ali a hand with the yoghurt and cheese making. Most of the produce was used on the farm, but some were sold in the farm shop, like fresh eggs, dairy products, potatoes, lettuces and punnets of seasonal fruit including mulberries from the ancient mulberry tree behind the stables.

May turned into June, then July and I felt I had never experienced such contentment and inner freedom. I worked hard, although I don't think the manual work of the farm produced much to keep the bills going. It was more Ali's coaching work that she carried out in the converted stable that kept us going. As a personal coach she had established an excellent reputation in helping people reframe the way they thought about themselves. This reframing would affect their businesses and creative enterprises, having a knock-on effect on the people around them.

"Why don't you come in and see what I do," Ali invited on

several occasions. "You don't have to do anything, just sit in and watch..."

I was torn. On one level I was curious to know how Ali worked with young business people, the obvious skill she had in invoking the will in individuals by unpicking the areas where it had become trapped. She was especially good with women who had grown up with strong dominant male figures and had deliberately culled their natural entrepreneur skills for fear of being bullied or disliked. Women would generally forge ahead in their twenties driven by their innate enthusiasm, becoming good at management, working with others and then at some point in their thirties, they would become bored, disillusioned with their achievements and go for another management position. Ali would, by her coaching skills, help them to unravel whether there was a genuine fear of success, or whether there was something else struggling to emerge into the foreground. Sometimes, she would suggest to her clients that management didn't hold enough excitement for them. Maybe they weren't realizing their full potential as the leader they believed they could never become. Management was a very different entity to Leadership. Management was working with other people, maintaining the status quo, working hard and diligently for set goals. The disappointment in this was whether the goals you were working hard to achieve and maintain were in line with your own inner vision. Ali would begin to slowly, painstakingly reveal and explore the distinctions between management and leadership. A leader took risks in a way that managers never did; were happy working on their own, enthused others around them with their ideals and dreams. Managers took up their positions around the mountain top, happy to be working with others and to be at the top. They were comfortable because they still had their feet on the ground. It was the leaders who foolishly, through manager's eyes, left the safe haven of structure and solidity and dared the heights. It was the leader that risked all for a vision and, yet, could inspire all the workers to serve that same vision and become inspired by it too. Ali had encountered many women who remained stationary in reliable moderately well paid management positions, but who had sacrificed their dreams, their soul even for fear of what they might lose or gain by moving forward. There were female leaders, maverick ones, who had dared to dream; entrepreneurs like Body Shop's Anita Roddick , Estee Lauder, Madame C J Walker Fields, the daughter of African slaves, orphaned at the age of seven, who created a successful beauty business employing 3000 people.

But the hesitation was in getting too involved in Ali's coaching work, even though she would have appreciated my support. I had already examined my feelings around this, wondering if fear or inadequacy was behind it. And I kept coming up with the same reason: now, didn't feel like the right time. It was as if I was waiting for another boat to come in.

Ali was always quick to support my decision. "Well, I do really appreciate your work around the farm," Ali pointed out. "My days of using the Rotavator and struggling with the tractor are over now…"

And Moo…

Well, Moo never stayed away for long. She was back after that unfortunate incident of the fleas; rubbing against me and purring as if I had never opened my clumsy mouth. But she did go missing for days on end. This worried me at first, until I was struck by how well she looked on her return. Unlike the expeditions she had taken to the Portal before my accident, she was returning from her sojourns smelling of honeysuckle and covered from head to tail with scented pollen. She was ecstatic, purring loudly and, if I didn't know Moo better, I'd wonder if she wasn't taking recreational drugs, or at least some form of exotic smelling catnip! Sometimes, it seemed as if Michael went with her, because he too would be heavily dusted with pollen and smelling fragrantly of one scent or another.

Often in the night, I would waken to the scent of some beautiful fragrance, rose, or freesia and there would be no Moo; just the indentations of her paws across the duvet, leaving a golden dust everywhere. This pollen dust would coat the dressing table and also the windowsills. Sometimes there were small clear drops of a honey-like substance that was sticky to touch and I also found that on the duvet. Whatever Moo was up to, it was sticky and yellow. Perhaps she had been rolling in the flowerbeds as cats sometimes do. I had to admit I had never experienced anything like it.

Patrick had noticed the sticky drops too on the furniture. "It's everywhere," he exclaimed. "I even found some of it on my football...What the heck is it?"

Ali examined it one breakfast. "Its nectar, it doesn't taste like honey, it's too raw..."

"Ugh! Mum!" Patrick exclaimed. "It could have been cat's pee...Or snot..."

"The thing is," Ali said, unperturbed. "It's all round the house, in my bedroom, in the bathroom – and there's pollen..."

"It must be the bees," I said.

Ali shook her head. "Bees rarely come in here, and the nectar would have to come from flowers or blossom. Aphids produce this sort of thing from the plants, but I'd expect to see ants around too, because they milk the aphids for the nectar."

"Ugh," from Patrick. "Milking aphids! That's gross!"

Just then Moo, who had been missing for several days, appeared in our midst, jumping up on the kitchen table, fur all fluffed out with a mixture of blossom and pollen. She mewed hungrily as we all stared at her.

"Moo!" Patrick exclaimed. "You're the culprit! Look at you, you're covered in it." He touched her. "Look at her tail and whiskers...It's like glue."

"What on earth have you been doing?" I chided Moo. "You're covered in this yellow pollen stuff and your fur's all sticky."

Moo, embarrassed by the way we were all staring accusingly at her, skedaddled out of the window and, later, I went after her, slipping a tin of tuna into my pocket along with a can opener.

I found Moo hiding behind the beehives, only made visible by the irritable twitching of her tail. "Moo," I began. "I know you're there...You don't have to hide, I'm not cross with you."

The tail began to twitch more violently. But then, as I opened the tin and emptied the contents onto the grass, Moo's powers of self-restraint gave way to her immediate needs and she lunged forward, giving a low growl as she laid her claim to the tuna meat. I waited patiently until Moo had eaten her fill, which amounted to over half the tin. Finally she drew breath and licked her paw so that she could dowse down her sweet fragrance with a more pervading fishy one.

I've been doing important work, she said at last.

"I know..." I offered gently. "I know you've been going where you have to go...It's just that..." How could I say this tactfully? "You do bring a lot of pollen and gluey stuff into the cottage...It's rather messy work and it's not making you very popular."

Moo continued washing, but had to stop every now and then as her tongue became coated with the sticky fur...*I come straight from the Portal. It's a by product of the work I do, like coal dust from the mines or paint from painting...*

"I'd like to go with you sometime Moo," the words slipped from my mouth before I could bite them back.

Moo's ears pricked and the paw she was washing hovered in mid air. *You want to go with me?* she echoed.

"Yes...If I may." I could hardly believe what I was saying.

It seemed then as if even the bees stopped buzzing, so great was the silence between us. *Of course you may,* Moo purred and her pleasure was like honey across my soul.

Anything that had fractured our relationship in the past, melted away as she came out from hiding and jumped up onto the seat beside me. *I've wanted you to come with me for so long,* Moo said. *It had to come from you. Everyone who enters the Portal enters of their own volition. But I have to tell you Peter, this Portal is very different to the other Portal, the one that the Nasym have broken through.*

"So I gather," I said. "You seem so deliriously happy each time you come back."

Yes, Moo agreed. *It's very healing because I'm returning to my source. And there's nothing to be afraid of…I don't have to be on my guard all the time!*

Now that the decision had been made, I concentrated on the logistics. "How do I get there though? Can humans enter a Portal like this – inside out?"

Moo smiled into my soul and as she did, I felt a wild stirring of excitement that I hadn't experienced since I was a young boy. It was a stirring that smacked of adventure and the unknown. Yet, it was as terrifying as it was seductive.

"Do humans go through the Portal?"

Not often, Moo responded and rubbed her sticky whiskers against my hand. *But it has been known. I have been longing for you to come, but we are not allowed to openly invite or suggest this to a human…*

"It's all about free will, isn't it?"

It's always about free will.

"The only thing is that you can go missing for days…How do I explain that to Ali? She would be worried and…"

You don't want to jeopardize your relationship with Ali, Moo finished.

"That's right…"

You won't…

"And I don't want to come back all covered in pollen and that gluey stuff."

You won't, she added more to herself than to me, *that's the only advantage of not having fur.*

Silence came between us and I felt myself relax a little. "So there's no real pressure – or format, I just come and go…"

Moo licked her paw slowly in the way she always did when she was thinking carefully about how to express herself. *There is a format.*

"Oh?"

You need to prepare by watching what you eat and drink…And also what you think.

"Oh, so I have to fast and meditate?"

I felt Moo's amusement like tiny effervescent bubbles exploding inside my mind.

No red meat, no alcohol. No violence to any living creature…Well, you're really all right there, because you don't eat any meat now, but it's important you prepare yourself and meditate.

"That's rich coming from you, Moo!" My words rushed out. "You kill mice, very violently."

I don't eat them…

"Nor do I! And we both eat tuna."

Moo's tail twitched. *I'm not perfect, Peter. I never said I was. But, you did ask a question, and I'm answering it…*Moo could be so irritating at times. *There has to be a purifying process before you go to this Portal, or else it will reject you. Spit you out.*

"Okay," I gave in. "When do we go?"

Soon.

I bit back a somewhat petulant, 'How soon?' and concentrated on more practical issues instead. "How big is the Portal? Can I fit through it?"

But of course! Moo laughed at this last question. *The Portal is infinite. How could you not fit through it?*

Moo then seemed to get bored and wandered off in the shade of the buddleia, which seemed to have drawn all the bees in the beehive into its fragrant colorful depths. I was left to wonder about the crazy decision I had made and whether I'd even recognize the Portal if it were to tap me on the shoulder.

My reverie by the beehives was cut short by Patrick hollering out that the goats had got loose and were making their way up the country lane towards the main road. This had happened before and caused a delivery van to plough through the hedge and puncture several tires in an effort to avoid them. Although, thankfully, no one was hurt, Ali was still wincing from the claim the driver's company had made against her for damages and loss of time. Ali hadn't dared claim against her own insurance for fear of losing her no claims bonus, in the event of something more catastrophic happening. Then there was the time only a month ago when the goats had made straight for the first village church fete of that year. Patrick and I had arrived red-faced and out of breath, just as the vicar was making an opening speech. While all attention was focused on the opening, the goats had found their way into the food marquise where all the homemade cakes, flans, chutneys, jams, scones and ice cream were on display. The two goats had been found in the urn of freshly whipped cream, tails wagging furiously as they gulped down the contents. If it had been just the fresh cream that had suffered, that at least would have been replaceable. But it was the collateral damage of nibbled awnings, the chewed tablecloth which they had brought down from one side of the table, the trampled flapjacks, fairy cakes with jelly, trifle and marmalade jars spilling their contents all over the floor.

A public apology was made amidst 'tuts tuts' from the ladies who had spent so much time preparing the tables and Ali had promised to return in the hour with fresh cream, cakes she had made for the summer and marmalade to replace the damage. Thankfully, because the sun was shining and the sky cloudless, promising an excellent day on the raffles, outside stalls and tombola, the vicar had taken the whole thing in good spirits. Pictures of the goats had been snapped up by a photographer from the local paper. Later, these same pictures had found their way into the Parish Newsletter. Additionally, the local paper were pleased to have a follow-up story on the two wayward goats together with a history of Buttercup Farm alongside photographs of its workers and inhabitants. The farm shop had sold out by noon every afternoon and people, at a loss what to do, asked to take pictures of the goats, which eventually found themselves on postcards and sold well in the farm shop and local newsagent.

Fortunately, we found the goats halfway down the lane, having already munched their way into John and Emily Rutland's rose garden, through the honeysuckle and lupins. The blood seemed to drain from my temples as Patrick found them heading for the season's prize roses. Wordlessly, with barely a glance at each other, Patrick and I slunk in, grabbed each goat by the rope and yanked them away forcefully, avoiding their vigorous head butting by steering them relentlessly forward and into the waiting Land Rover. I spent the rest of the day strengthening and reinforcing their enclosure. We made a pact not to tell Ali about the goats' misadventure and cause her any unnecessary concern. She was on good terms with the Rutlands and they regularly purchased her dairy products and, recently, their grandson had recommended a number of people to her training courses. This regular addition to her coaching program was freeing up enough income to renovate the last barn and prevent it falling into disuse. And although she wasn't sure what the renovated barn could be utilized for, she knew it would be an investment, either to lease out to people on a short term or permanent basis. If Ali knew the goats had begun to rampage the Rutlands' precious rose garden, she would never have been able to keep it a secret. Good friendships were culled on a lot less grounds than two charging goats. Ali needed all the local support she could get. Besides, there were plenty of wild deer around and, if nothing was said, the Rutlands would put it down to them.

After reinforcing the fence and returning the goats to safe ground, milking the cows and collecting the eggs for Patrick as he was having a sleepover at Georgie's, I was once again wondering where time had gone. What had begun as an early morning communion with Moo, had become late morning and then early afternoon. I would have to rustle up some supper in the form of a salad and flan for Ali, since she would be finishing her late session with her students soon.

"How's it been?" she asked, giving me a hug and pressing her cheek against mine. "Has it been a good day for you?"

"Oh you know," I said, hugging her back. "There's never a dull moment on a farm…"

"Tell me about it!" She sank down next to me on the seat under the willow. "Are you still happy here?"

"I am, Ali…I never thought I would be cut out to do this manual labor – but I actually enjoy it…In this weather, anyway. I just…" I broke off and looked into the far distance.

"You just what?" Ali returned gently.

"I feel guilty that I'm not doing enough. Not pulling my weight."

Ali dropped a kiss onto my cheek. "Without you, I wouldn't be able to work as I do…What the heck would I do without you? I saw what you did today, erecting that fence to keep the goats in. A hired help costs a fortune."

"I feel I should be doing more – more with my life," I said.

She slipped her hand in mine and I realized how comfortable and right that felt.

"I know that feeling and I understand it. You sound as if you're in that state which Buddhists refer to as Bardo, the liminal place between states of consciousness."

"Go on," I encouraged.

"Well, there are supposed to be six of these Bardo states…The first takes place when we are born, the second when we dream, the third when we meditate…Then there's a fourth when we die…This is followed by one of luminosity and the sixth of transmigration…But there are smaller Bardos within the template of our single lifetime. Liminal states where new opportunities and conditions are waiting to emerge…The more you try to push and make things happen, the more it inhibits the natural working out of what is struggling to be born…. The best way to manage it is to take it all lightly… hang loose… and just go with it."

Although I knew this to be true, I still fretted about it. "I feel as if I've been here in this 'Bardo' months, not weeks," I said.

"You know what I think?" Ali began, flicking her hair back from her face. "I think your proud critical male is in full force today…. He wants to be the provider because he resides in cultural injunctions that sustain this belief…. It's hard for that male to take a back seat."

"You're right," I said squeezing her hand. "I'm just feeling very guilty… But tell me about that Bardo luminosity state…"

"Well – it's what you experience after death, but we both know that death isn't just death of the physical body…. It's death of dreams, of a way of life, of a belief system." She smiled. "In other words, if you allow it to happen, you could realise some of that spiritual luminosity."

Later, after lunch, Ali took me to the barn she had been talking about.

Although I had known it was there beyond the grove of yew trees, I'd resisted an urge to have a peek at it, feeling that it was a secret place that Ali would show me in her own time.

The evening had cooled as Ali led me across the courtyard, through the hazel copse towards the yew grove to where the old barn stood. These yews, she explained proudly, have been here hundreds of years. Long before the farm was built.

"History tells us that they were once used by Druids," she explained. "But somebody found some ancient unpublished manuscript about it in an old relative's dressing table…About it being a place where witches had met and performed healing rites for clans-people. The manuscript had even hinted at spirit travel…"

A chill ran through me as I remembered what Moo had told me about the witches and how their original meeting places had been in oak and yew groves.

Briefly, as I glanced behind me, I caught sight of Moo trotting behind us from a distance, ever curious to explore new territory and see what we were getting up to. It loomed up in front of us, higher than the other barns while house martins and swallows laid claim to their cupped nests under the eaves.

"Come on in," Ali invited.

The barn smelt and felt ancient, sacred all at the same time. Ali stepped inside and offered her hand to me. "Come on," she invited. "Are you up for a little exploring?"

I'd expected it to be dark inside the building, but light swept through an opening where a couple of roof tiles had fallen in. The temporary polyurethane cladding used as a stopgap had fallen into a muddy weathered heap onto the ground.

Momentarily, I was mesmerized by the shaft of sunlight, the motes of dust pouring across it, and somewhere, from a short while back, this image was overlaid by another...Of souls rising up and up into a scintillating vastness from the depths of a catastrophic brokenness below. But the light was strong. It ran like a river through the broken places in China where the earthquake had been...Burma where the cyclone had reached...Haiti...

Ali pulled the cladding aside and sank down on one of the hale bales, pulling me down beside her.

"How old is it?" I asked.

"In a word – ancient. No one knows how old it is. Some say it was even created by the Knights Templar and it was one of the places they used to meet for worship. My grandfather believed that this could have been built on the site of a Temple once."

"I can believe that."

We were talking in whispers as if the very walls of the building had reached out to silence us. In fact, the silence was so deep as to be almost deafening. "I wanted to bring you here because…"

I put a finger to her lips. "Ali…I have to say this," my heart was knocking like a castanet as the words tumbled out, uncontrollably, "but, I think I love you…"

Silence rushed in on us and feelings that had, until then, been all tamped down, silenced into submission for fear of loss, clamored to be recognized.

Ali's mouth found mine; hungry, searching, and I didn't care any more about fears and restraints. Suddenly, our bodies were naked and Ali's skin a golden glow as the rays of sun found us. The sun's rays were scalding as though unleashed from a potter's kiln. We were seized by longings deeper than we knew, primeval ones that may have belonged to this place or been dislodged within the furnace of our own need. Her skin beneath my hands, her lips warm caramel on my tongue. Deeper, we explored, consumed each other, caramel giving way to musk and salt as breast ran into nipple, navel and the most sensual depths between her thighs. We groaned as we entered each other and I cried, or she yelped, as we rode each other. She was so deep and I could not hold back and we were riding each other, over and over and under. Heat upon heat rose up inside us, between us and still we pushed, holding that peak like a great wave, poised…Poised…Not breaking and…There was no separation. We were two sides of the same skin. Blindly, I wondered where each of us began and ended.

"Ali…My love…"

A cry from her or me, but I was riding on, and that light which was pouring through the broken ceiling was inside my skull. Blinding brilliance, and the smell of sweet hay became the scent of honeysuckle. Falling and falling like a golden rain around me was gold dust, pollen…The air tasted sweet, not just to my tongue, but to my senses.

There was pollen everywhere; not sticky like plant honeydew, but a fine powder, which filmed everything. And at first, distantly, the humming more insistent as if there were thousands of tiny pneumatic drills at work...But then the sound became deeper and I found myself standing before a huge cavernous backdrop of glittering, pulsing light. The stars moved, and seemed to break away into individual impressions of gossamer wings.

I blinked and shielded my eyes at the sight before me. A sight such as I had never seen or imagined before, not even my wildest dreams. Yet it was enough to stop the heart...And I knew then that I had, at long last, entered the Portal.

Soul Rocks is a fresh list that takes the search for soul and spirit mainstream. Chick-lit, young adult, cult, fashionable fiction & non-fiction with a fierce twist.